The Summerfield Stories

The Summerfield Stories

by
J.M. Ferguson, Jr.

Texas Christian University Press
Fort Worth

Copyright © 1985 by J. M. Ferguson, Jr.

Library of Congress Cataloging in Publication Data
Ferguson, J. M. (Joseph M.)
The Summerfield stories.
I. Title.
PS3556.E713S8   1985   813'.54   84-16443
ISBN 0-87565-000-7
ISBN 0-87565-010-4 (pbk.)

Designed by WHITEHEAD & WHITEHEAD
Jacket painting by Joe M. Ferguson, Sr.

The Morning Hours, Spending the Day, Summerfield, The Changes and
Enemies in the City appeared originally in *Descant*. *The Walking Stick*
appeared originally in *Arizona Quarterly*.

The Summerfield Stories

To the memory of my father and my son, and,
with love, for those who loved them

"In some of us a child—lost, strayed off the beaten path—goes wandering to the end of time while we, in another garb, grow up, marry or seduce, have children, hold jobs, or sit in movies, and refuse to answer our mail."
—Loren Eiseley, The Night Country

The Morning Hours

*I*F YOU HAVE AN EYE FOR ITS PARTICULAR VASTNESS AND beauty, the northeast quarter of New Mexico is a country which will yet strike you as strangely neglected. The land is desert with a touch of prairie, or prairie with a strong hint of desert, depending on its mood, and your own, and where you're from. Cross it going east toward Texas and you see a continent leveling out, rolling slightly or sometimes abruptly, broken here and there by volcanic butte and bluff and ravine. Head west and follow the road to San Anselmo, as my family did years ago, and the long thread of the highway will bring you to that eventual rise where, if it be summer, you peer over a little wilderness of gazing sunflowers on the blue mountains of the Sangre de Cristo range. But look up, from wherever you happen to be standing on that wide mesa, and you behold the source of the land's enchantment. Vast enough to be moody and sunlit at the same time, this sky imparts to the land its peace or its passion, but always its grandeur. In summer piles of cloud, fierce and sunburned, are almost always adrift there, yet never seeming to consume the vastness of the blue they drift in, making you feel that you have forever.

In my memories of that country the sky is always blue, and the cottonwoods along the river are turning autumnal gold. In the mountains, my father and I fished the clear running streams in the high meadows. Sometimes my father packed his water colors, and I can remember a New Mexican farmer or two strolling across his irrigation fields to exchange his few words of English with us and smile with recognition at my father's landscape. Without really knowing it, I loved the quick odor of stream and field, the earth and air of those shadowless days, the morning hours of my life.

Our frame and white stucco house sat among a few scattered companions near the bottom of a low, treeless ridge north of town. My father, who was teaching art at the high school in San Anselmo, rattled up and down the dusty washboard road in our 1926 Chevrolet. He had painted it gunmetal gray in his esteem for it after our safe migration from far away West Virginia. I remember myself as a schoolboy, as often as not late for supper because I had played too long at sandlot baseball, pumping my bicycle up that same road, slowly, in the face of biting winds. For when spring storms finally came—and they could be sudden and violent—the wind whistled through the mouth of the mountains and shook the house, piling sand in the yard and tumbleweeds against the wall below the windows.

One afternoon while digging in that sand and loam behind our house, I uncovered a Spanish spur. I remember it was mostly brass, but attached to it and meant to circle the heel of some forgotten boot was a leather thong which had turned black and begun to rot even in the dry New Mexico sand.

I was still a year too young for school when we moved into that small white house. My father had provided me with Blackjack, a black and tan terrier whose ancestry was otherwise undeterminable. He was smart and game, and his presence proved a calamity for the lizards in the immediate area. Yet in spite of his companionship, I remember vividly my hours of loneliness. My few playmates were older than I and got tired of seeing me around, and I was left to swordfight with my own shadow, until finally I would retire to the shade of the backdoor steps and sink into contemplation, my elbows on my knees and my head between my hands.

I was in such an attitude, I believe, when Skipper Summerfield first appeared in my life, peeping between the blood-red hollyhocks which my mother had growing along the fence that separated our yard from the mesa beyond. Miraculously, it seemed to me, this perfect companion had arrived in our neighborhood, and but for an incident or two which caused us momentary separations, we were together so much from that day that people in San Anselmo began to mistake us for brothers. We worked out a signal, a whistled refrain which could be heard across the fields between our houses, by which we summoned one another at any hour of the day. We fought day-long tin-soldier battles on the sandy ridges behind our houses, and we took long hikes on the mesa, packing the lunches our mothers had prepared, "fishing" with homemade poles for tumbleweeds in the dry arroyos. He had a coal-black retriever named Jake, and after some initial uneasiness in each other's presence, even our dogs decided to tolerate each other for the sake of keeping us company.

I recall a photograph of the four of us together which my father snapped one day. Skipper is astride Jake, pony-soldier style, and I'm on one knee with my arm around Blackjack. Both dogs are smiling, the way dogs can smile, with their mouths open panting and their tongues lapped over their teeth.

I believe that it was later that year, not long after his picture was taken, that Blackjack came to an untimely death. One cold winter night as the wind buffeted the house, I heard him at the back door. He barked once, a feeble, hollow sound that echoed disturbingly in my thoughts that night. I made no move to let him in, knowing my father forbade him in the house, and

3

knowing the garage door, as always, was propped open for him. But next morning the story was plain enough. We found him dead, poisoned, beside the hydrant in back of the house. He had come home poisoned, barked just once, and died alone.

We buried him in a far corner of the yard. I have often wished I had opened the door that night, that I had been with him when he died. And I have wondered whether I would have had the courage, alone in the cold of a winter night, to die as well.

San Anselmo was growing, and across the street and down the way from us another new family had arrived in the neighborhood. The father—I remember him simply as Mr. Montoya—opened a small grocery in the town. He was a kind and patient man, and this was well, for his one son, Eddie, was often the object of persecution among his childhood acquaintances. Eddie bore an obvious birthmark on his right temple, and, just as obvious and perhaps more cruel, he stammered painfully whenever he spoke.

I don't think I ever saw Eddie's mother—I'm not even sure he had one—but I always liked his father. His straight black hair, his countenance and his patience suggested at least a trace of Indian blood in his veins. Time after time, when Eddie went home rejected, crying with his feelings hurt, I would see his father come out in the yard to meet and console him. He never said an angry word or gave the offenders an angry glance, but he would talk with Eddie and play with him until he had him in good spirits again. Then he always tried to get him to go back to his playmates, and if he could not, he would carry him piggyback into the house. He was the only person who ever showed any kindness to Eddie.

Mr. Montoya spoke pleasantly to everyone. In his store I sometimes heard him speak rapidly in Spanish to native New Mexicans, but he spoke English with careful fluency to Anglos like myself, and it was a source of some embarrassment to me when, leaving his store one day with Skipper Summerfield, I heard Skipper mock his rapid Spanish in nonsense syllables, but in a voice which I feared must have been audible to the storekeeper.

I'll never know whether he overheard us, but even if he did, we were guilty of a subsequent act which must have hurt him infinitely more. I had, in the interim, reproached Skipper bitterly, and it was then, I believe, that he had put the idea into my head that it was Mr. Montoya who had poisoned my dog. He attached the blame to him solely on the grounds that Mr. Montoya was the newcomer to the neighborhood, and although I protested, I confess that for awhile thereafter I saw him with resentment in my eye.

Then one day as we were on our sandhill, busy scouting Indians, I saw Eddie and his father get out of their car across the road. Eddie was carrying a package under his arm when they went into their house, and a few minutes later he emerged wearing short pants and brand new cowboy boots. Galloping toward us, he stammered with excitement, "Look at me, I'm a cowboy, I'm a cowboy!"

I don't know whether it was resentment for the demise of Blackjack, jealousy over the new boots, or just a lust for excitement that made us do it, and I don't recall which of us acted first, but we stood up at his approach, our hands full of gravel, and began an assault on his bare legs. "Whoever heard of a cowboy in short pants," I shouted. "Just tell me whoever heard of such a thing!"

With an animal-like expression of surprise and hurt, Eddie turned and staggered home behind a profusion of tears. We dropped all the gravel from our hands and faced each other, suddenly sick with shame, and I looked over and saw Eddie's father coming out to meet him, talking softly as always. But he never did get him cheered up again that day, and when he finally had to take him into the house Eddie was still crying. About a week later there was a moving van in front of their house, and when it pulled away Mr. Montoya and his son disappeared quietly and forever from San Anselmo.

There followed one of those rare intervals when Skipper Summerfield and I remained apart. When I did see him again, several weeks after the Montoyas had moved, he came with tears in his eyes to tell me Jake had been poisoned.

The ownership of Mr. Montoya's little grocery was assumed by a rather plump and self-satisfied man named Schwartz. I took him for a Californian, for in the one clear picture I retain of him he's standing behind his counter, scooping handfuls of coins from two cylindrical quart containers and sifting them lustily between his fingers, crowing "I got barrels of this stuff out in California."

As a boy still too young to know better I came home from his store one day with a loaf of bread I had been sent for, but badly short-changed. My father was furious; it was the midst of the depression, and though I can't remember that we ever suffered for it, I suppose that we had little to spare. He confronted Mr. Schwartz and recovered his loss without delay, and I would like to think it was owing to this incident rather than to any inherent prejudice on our part—in San Anselmo we Anglos were ourselves a minority—but thereafter, between Skipper Summerfield and myself, Mr. Schwartz bore the epithet of "Jew Baby."

It was a terrible, unfortunate phrase that we somehow harbored for years almost unwittingly, and even though I came to wince a little when it appeared unpredictably, it nonetheless persisted. "Be careful, Sonny," my mother would say. "You'll be sorry someday." She was a charitable woman. She attended the Methodist church in San Anselmo with scrupulous regularity, and for the most part she did so alone, for on Sunday mornings my father insisted on meeting with his own "regulars" at the public courts for his weekly game of tennis, and I was prone to keep him company.

I was about fifteen, I believe, and I have long since forgotten the conversation which prompted it, but I found on my lips that carelessly sustained bit of acrimony, "Jew Baby," as we were seated about the dinner table one warm spring evening with Skipper Summerfield as our guest. "Be careful, Sonny," my mother warned. "Howard will hear you."

There followed one of those uncanny coincidences such as have visited me only two or three times in my life, but as she was cautioning me the doorball rang. I knew that the front door stood open, that there was only a screen door to shield us from our caller. As I moved to answer the bell I prayed to myself that it wouldn't be Howard, or, since I knew somehow that it was, that he hadn't heard. But by the time I saw his face, I knew that he had.

The man to whom my mother had referred was Howard Rosensweig. No one knew what Howard did for his living, or where he had come from. I thought at first that he was perhaps another of San Anselmo's tubercular or asthmatic exiles from the East—my father and I both fell into the latter category—but in time I came to realize his afflictions were more of the mind or heart. A lanky man with a mop of curly brown hair, he walked with a slight stoop to his shoulders, and as I watched him stroll forlornly on his twilight walks up and down our main street, the highway that was beginning to see its share of the traffic of a continent shuttle back and forth, I began to discern something indefinably pathetic about the man. It was nothing physical, but what I can best describe in retrospect as a kind of spiritual limp.

On Sunday mornings Howard appeared at the tennis courts for months before anyone realized he could play. Neatly dressed and drawing on his pipe, he sat on a bench behind the court and watched reflectively for the most part, but I believe it was during

7

this time that he first struck up a speaking acquaintance with some of the players, including my father. Then one morning he appeared in his tennis clothes—he always wore white duck slacks when he played; I never saw Howard in a pair of shorts. It may have been our fine autumn weather which drew him out, but when my father asked him to play it was discovered soon enough that San Anselmo had another "regular."

Howard never talked about where he had played before— or, for that matter, about his past at all—but it was soon observed that he played nothing but doubles, declining all invitations to singles on the grounds that he hadn't "the wind for it." In truth, I believe, Howard didn't have the heart for the really competitive game, and I noticed that even in doubles he was careful to choose a partner of less ability than himself, someone who, like himself, did not mind losing. In the years when I was learning to play, I was myself his frequent partner, and it was only on these occasions that, perhaps for my sake, he seemed at all interested in the business of winning or losing. He taught me a great deal on the court, for he was a fine player, as anyone who saw him standing on a court warming up would agree. Yet once in a match he seemed never very interested in pressing an advantage—a trait which I cannot help attributing now to a kind of compassion he had for his opponents and indeed for the world of men. Had it not been for the mellow autumn sun which first lured him onto our courts, I am sure he would have preferred to remain a spectator on the bench behind the backstop, pipe in hand, watching us with his warm but essentially sad eyes.

At the bottom of the road that ran out by our house, where it joined the highway that passed through San Anselmo, Howard lived in a room at the Modern Court—no one had yet heard the term "motel" in that day, and the Modern Court was what was referred to as a tourist court, being among the less luxurious of the several in San Anselmo. One summer Howard took to plodding up the dusty road to visit us following his customary twilight strolls. He seemed to enjoy our company, and on one occasion was even prevailed upon by my mother to stay for dinner. At night, from my bedroom at the back end of the house, I more than once heard Howard and my father talking about art in the garage which my father had converted to his studio. I gathered Howard knew something about the subject, for I detected a rare hint of excitement in his voice.

When school started again Howard knew that my father was busy at the high school, and his visits became less frequent. At midwinter they stopped altogether, and, at about the same time, I began to miss him on Sundays at the tennis courts. Confiding to me one day that something my father had said led her to believe that he and Howard had quarreled, my mother asked me what I knew about it, but if they had I had been unaware of the incident. Yet I knew that for a sensitive man my father could also be reckless. His quarrels with my mother were never violent but sometimes bitter, and I believe he took his violence out in other ways; behind the wheel of the old Chevy, for example, he sometimes drove like a man intoxicated, though he never drank. Still later, my mother told me she had heard that Howard was ill and sent me off to him with a pot of her homemade soup.

It was a Saturday morning and the scent of spring was in the air, but Howard's room, I recall, struck me as the abode of a man who didn't care. It was musty and crumpled, and an odor of stale tobacco mingled with another which was unfamiliar to me but unwholesome. Howard was dressed, but I gathered from the appearance of his clothes and his bed that he had been lying down. He looked pale and he spoke thickly and moved heavily, yet he was as cordial and kind as ever. He thanked me profusely for the soup and made me promise twice to thank my mother. Seeing the baseball mitt I had strapped to my belt, he tried to make some conversation with me about the Brooklyn Dodgers. They were his favorite team, he said, and it was the only hint I ever had about his origins. While we talked I noticed, scratched on the back of an envelope on his bedside table, what I took to be a poem, but what attracted me most was Howard's sole attempt at decoration in the room. Above the bed, taped to the wall I sat facing, was a print of a Rembrandt portrait, a muted and moody painting of a man in a gold helmet. There was beauty in the man's face, or, more accurately perhaps, a sensitivity to what was beautiful, what was just, but in that same face I read world-weariness and infinite disappointment.

It must have been not long after that day that Howard, somewhat recovered, hobbled up to our house for what proved to be the last time. Needless to say, he pretended that he hadn't overheard what I had recklessly blurted to my friend Skipper Summerfield at the dinner table that evening. Yet, as I've said, his face betrayed only too plainly that he had. He made a little conversation, returned the soup bowl to my mother with elaborate thanks, and as he plodded away again with his enigmatic limp, I could tell he was deeply hurt.

I was greatly ashamed, of course, and some days later I again made my way down to Howard's room at the Modern Court, having resolved finally that an apology might be better than nothing at all. But the room, to my mingled disappointment and relief, was no longer Howard's, and in the window the landlord had placed a sign: "Vacancy, weekly or monthly rates."

I hung about the house that day in a dark mood until my mother asked what was troubling me. She knew well enough, but she wanted to give me a chance to talk about it. When I told her, she searched my face for a long minute. Then, faintly emphasizing the verb, as if to suggest it was something he must have willed upon himself, as if to share with me her disbelief, she told me ever so softly, "Howard died."

The editor of San Anselmo's daily had called her to ask what we knew about Howard, and finding we could add nothing about his background, had explained that his death would be noted simply in the weekly obituary column.

I waited another long minute, and said, "He was from Brooklyn, I think," as if for the information of the newspaper editor as well as my mother. Then, turning my back and burning to be out of her sight, I added cruelly, "And I wish to God he'd stayed there."

I outlasted my guilt, or whatever it was I was feeling at the time. Skipper Summerfield and I graduated from high school together, and then, while he went East to college, I spent four years at the state university in Southwest City. I played varsity tennis, and once in awhile I thought about Howard Rosensweig, but not for long. I was young, and I wanted to be a poet.

I also survived the war, and, feeling compelled to do so, made my pilgrimage to San Anselmo. I had never been so aware of, or moved by, that country's enduring beauty. I could not imagine it ever changing, and yet it had changed subtly for me, or more likely, I for it.

Survivor of myself, I tried to describe what it was about the land that so affected me. I hit upon something I would never have come to before, and when I had done that, my feeling of forever that that part of the earth had always imparted to me began to evaporate. The characteristic I speak of, the one which I finally decided was at the bottom of that land's power to move the heart of the man who wandered over it, was its timeless innocence.

Spending the Day

*H*ARRY SUMMERFIELD WASN'T REALLY HARRY AND HIS WIFE Ida wasn't really Ida. He detested his given name and was aware that Ida only used it when he had prodded her to vindictiveness. And he was tired of the childish nickname which had long concealed the given name, so these were just names that came to Harry one fall day while they were driving along in the Sierras in their little blue Chevy with their blue-eyed daughter. Blue was Harry's favorite color. His own blue eyes, however, were often bloodshot now. He claimed they were a symptom of his anxiety, a condition that had plagued him strangely since the war. Ida had once suggested, gently, that he was tending toward hypochondria.

"Who would you rather be," he had blurted as they climbed through Tioga Pass into Yosemite, "Edna or Ida Mae?"

"For Christ's sake, Merton," Ida sighed. "Do you have to start that stuff?"

Harry had an irrepressible way of coming up with questions that annoyed Ida.

"Which?" he insisted.

"Ida, I guess."

"Just call me Harry," Harry said. "I've always wanted to be Harry."

"Christ, Merton. You and Harry Truman."

It was true, of course, that Harry was an ardent Democrat. Before the war he had gone with Ida to Kentucky to meet her parents, and when he had ventured his admiration for F. D. R. Ida's father had turned red around the neck and ordered him out of the house. Years later, naming their daughter had caused a family crisis. Harry had wanted to name her Eleanor after Eleanor Roosevelt. "A great lady," he explained. But Ida had once known an Eleanor whom she detested, and besides her father had voted Republican for forty years. So they named the baby Elaine, which Harry suggested as a compromise. It seemed to Harry that his life was composed of just such compromises.

"Harry and Ida," Harry murmured without satisfaction, his finger in his nose.

It was late September, and at that altitude the leaves on the aspen were already turning. The car had begun to descend into Yosemite Valley, and they had dropped into a rolling mist that was infiltrating the great pines. Harry really didn't know why he said such absurd things. He was a poet by nature and next to being Harry he would have preferred to be called Homer. A hawk was circling above them, and Harry could see that Ida was watching it, her face pressed sadly against the car window.

"Harry and Ida," he said again, flatly. And the names had stuck.

When Harry and Ida were married the war was already on in Europe. They lived in a small walkup apartment near the university where Harry was struggling with his graduate work. Ida's father had disowned her. They were poor and neither of them was used to it. Harry made the first months of their marriage miserable with his complaining and Ida went home in the third month.

Harry decided to be grateful for the experience of cohabiting with a woman. It gave him a new perspective on things and made his poetry seem like the purest drivel. He decided to call it growth on his part. He watched the moon drop down his window and walked to his classes under the bare winter trees and thought he could always be happy in his celibacy. But then one night he dreamed about a girl he thought he had forgotten. Tall and blonde, she was his kind of girl. Harry had dated her briefly in his undergraduate days, and he had fancied he was in love, but then one night she had turned suddenly cold to him. Harry never knew why.

Ida was back after a week. Her father had turned red around the neck and told her to lie in the bed she had made. Harry received her gracefully.

"Who would you rather be," he asked quietly, "Ralph Waldo Emerson or Henry David Thoreau?"

Ida looked at him queerly.

"Why?" she asked.

"I dunno," Harry said. "Thoreau never married."

"Henry David Thoreau, then," Ida said.

Harry nodded silently.

As it turned out they both got their wish. Harry's graduate career was broken off before he could finish his dissertation on Henry David Thoreau. It was the year of Pearl Harbor and Harry was drafted by midterm.

Ida cried when she saw him off on the train for his induction. Harry was touched. He didn't see her again for five years.

Harry came home from the war looking tired and, of course, older. He had been unfaithful to Ida during his last year overseas. He had picked up a girl in the Soho district of London on the day Roosevelt died, but he did not tell Ida. His eyes were bloodshot, and Ida remarked, as tactfully as she could, on his disgusting new habit of picking his nose. Harry explained it all as a symptom of his anxiety.

He sometimes had the uneasy feeling, looking into her steady gray eyes, that she was uncanny. She seemed to have divined his infidelity, and Harry could see she had suffered during his absence. She had supported herself as a waitress, and she too looked tired and older.

Harry couldn't face any more graduate school. He felt obliged to help his widowed mother. She had always been jealous of Ida and was especially so when she learned that Ida was expecting. He took a job in a teachers' college out west. He spent his small savings on a used Studebaker, but it broke down before they got there, and Harry had to borrow from the college credit union to buy the blue Chevy. Later he had to borrow more when the baby was born.

But their first year at the teachers' college was no improvement over graduate school. There was never enough money, and when Harry was home he sat over a stack of papers to be graded, rolling his eyes distractedly and fingering his nose. Ida became nervous and started to smoke a lot, and when Harry came home he found loaded ash trays scattered all over the house. He couldn't get the smell out of his head at night and slept fitfully. Somewhere along the line, he feared, she had come to blame him for something, and when he stopped to think about it, he couldn't really blame her in turn.

"I'm going to finish college when I get the chance," Ida would sometimes say. "We've got to have another income."

Harry sometimes caught himself thinking it was too bad they let women go to college—except for some of those in his classes, of course. Sometimes he would try to explain to Ida about education.

"That's not the point of education," he would begin, but the further his argument went, the more feeble it seemed to become. For a while he thought he would write a long philosophical paper on education, but he wore himself out thinking about it, and he sank listlessly into depression whenever he thought of all the people who were already writing papers about education. So finally Harry quit trying to explain.

They were both restless, and almost as soon as the baby was old enough they took to driving in the mountains on the weekends. But Ida made the mistake of saying she missed the blue grass.

"Blue grass your ass," Harry retorted one morning before they had gotten out of bed. He rather liked Montana.

In the end, however, they went back east for Harry to work on his doctorate again. Harry thought he really wanted to be a poet, but he knew he wasn't writing any poetry. It was one of Harry's compromises.

"Which would you rather be," he asked Ida on the way back, "a two thousand pound Montana grizzly or a Kentucky thoroughbred eating blue grass?"

"For Christ's sake, Merton," Ida sighed.

Harry had his finger in his nose and his eyes were bloodshot.

Harry began to allude to his "split personality" as he worked on his doctorate. He tried to explain that he didn't want to be a scholar but a poet.

"Go ahead and quit then," Ida would say, "but it's me you really want to get away from. I won't stop you if you do."

Harry would have gone, too, but it broke his heart to think of parting from Elaine. She had Ida's dark hair but Harry's blue and sensitive eyes, and Harry couldn't bear to desert her. He felt sorry for her. She seemed to be a nervous child and Harry feared she was developing asthma, an affliction he had endured in his own childhood. Ida said he was imagining, but Harry felt guilty about it.

Harry noticed that his handwriting had begun to change. Sometimes, for example, he would print the letter s, which he had never done before. But only sometimes, and without rhyme or reason, as far as he could see. Then he noticed that the same schizophrenia afflicted his capital D's and I's. Ida bought a paperback book on handwriting at the supermarket, but her only observation was a reluctant conclusion that Harry's r's indicated he was conceited.

It wasn't the handwriting itself, however, that disturbed Harry. He began to attribute his confusion to some frightening indecision and purposelessness in his character. The more he studied at the university the more often he found his meagre collection of convictions untenable, and Harry felt that he needed some convictions to sustain his identity. After all, he thought, wasn't it asinine to be confident about how to make s's when he did not know why he was bothering to make them at all? Distraction upon distraction seemed to prevent him from discovering the real answers. He felt that he was a man torn in two, but he didn't mention his handwriting to Ida again.

What he said instead was "I'm a man torn in two," and he read a passage from a book to her: "'Let us spend one day as deliberately as Nature, and not be thrown off the track by every nutshell and mosquito's wing that falls on the rails.' You know who that is?"

"Who?" Ida sighed.

"That's Henry David Thoreau," Harry beamed.

"Christ, Merton. You and Henry David Thoreau." Harry had been quoting Thoreau to her while he was writing his dissertation on him. "You really want to be Henry David Thoreau? Then go be Henry David. I won't stop you."

Ida was always saying something like that, but Harry knew he drove her to it, just as things were driving him in turn. He had read somewhere that his habit of fingering his nose was a symptom of his need for identity, and that there were certain sexual implications in it. He didn't know what Ida meant by her allusions to a habit of rolling his eyes, though.

Ida was smoking more than ever and had begun to cough, and whenever Harry would taunt that she was going to smoke herself to death she would sigh and say she wished she could.

"Well," Harry once replied, "I'm not sure what you mean by that, but it sure as hell sounds like you're accusing me of something."

Ida was about to offer a rejoinder, but before she could Harry began to beat his head with his fists. To his added bewilderment, however, Ida tried to restrain him, coughing and crying, telling him she was sorry about always wishing she were dead—she didn't really mean it—and that everything would be better when he could finish up the degree.

But in his heart of hearts Harry didn't believe everything would be better at all. Sometimes, sitting up alone at night, he was torn between working on his degree and writing a poem he had been nursing along in his head. He could do nothing but finger his nose. It was at such a moment one night that he caught himself rolling his eyes.

Harry never did finish his doctorate, and things didn't get better. He dragged his family west again and took a job in one of the California junior colleges he had heard about. He told Ida he could finish his dissertation "in absentia," which was a lie, and that they could move anywhere she liked when he did, which, of course, was also a lie.

The pay was better than it had been at the teachers' college, and Ida, looking tired and weary, was able to resign herself to her new surroundings except, it seemed, on Friday nights, the nights Harry liked to relax after a hard week of teaching. One such night Ida didn't get supper on the table until ten o'clock, and when she did Harry declined to eat it and spent the night at his office. He didn't have much heart for his teaching, either, and he found himself taking to girlwatching on campus. He often toyed with the idea of being single, but he would always end by thinking about his daughter. She was then nearly four years old and definitely asthmatic, Harry thought.

Harry tried to cheer Ida up whenever he could on the weekends by driving her to scenic points around California in their little blue Chevy, and it was during one of these trips, to Yosemite, that Harry thought of the names, Harry and Ida. He recognized that these outings were an escapist impulse, the same habit they had fallen into in Montana. On one trip, in an out-of-the-way green valley between some mountains, a man working with a hoe near the road raised his dusty face as they drove by and showed them a healthy animal smile. Harry couldn't get the man out of his mind. He made him think of some of D. H. Lawrence's characters. He knew their little excursions were only temporary stays—from what, he was not sure—and he was usually anxious about a stack of themes left behind that had to be graded. He felt his life slipping through his fingers while he drugged his spirit with the beautiful scenery.

"Who would you rather be," Harry blurted one Sunday afternoon while the sun was going down, "Henry David Thoreau or Lady Chatterley's lover?"

"Christ, Merton," Ida sighed. "Watch the road."

Harry quit his job abruptly in the middle of his second year at the junior college. He never offered any explanations. He came home one afternoon mumbling something incoherent in a hollow-sounding voice and flopped into a chair with his finger up his nose. Ida questioned him, but Harry only said, "I have nothing to teach." That was all she could get out of him.

Ida suspected Harry was having an affair. They had been to a party not long before, and she had seen him slap a willowy blonde on the buttocks. Harry had drunk himself into oblivion on the better part of a fifth of Jim Beam and gone around telling everyone he was throwing his hat into the ring for the presidency. He cited some Chief Justice that Ida had never heard of as a distant cousin. It was election year and Harry Truman had announced his plans to retire.

Harry found employment as a technical writer for a corporation in Sacramento that was doing secret defense work for the government. He had to pass a security clearance to get the job. He found the work boring and the routine tedious, but he was beyond caring and never complained. He realized there were easier ways to make money than teaching or writing poetry, and he began to work overtime on Saturdays. Ida suspected something was amiss.

She heard what it was from the wife of Harry's supervisor. Harry had been working overtime one Saturday when his supervisor caught him fornicating in a broom closet with one of his secretaries. Harry made allusions to his anxiety, but he didn't try to deny it. Both he and the secretary were dismissed, of course, as poor security risks, and again Harry's job had ended suddenly.

Ida took Elaine and went back to the blue grass country to look for a job as a waitress—for the better part of her life, it seemed to her, she'd been waiting for Harry. Harry found himself alone, divorced, and saddled with a judgment for child support. He was still carrying the debts he had incurred at the teachers' college, transferring them from one credit union to another as he moved about.

It seemed to Harry that the world was being run by Republicans, who had won the November elections. And he felt guilty about Elaine.

Harry did his best to pull himself together. He had long nourished a secret desire to be single again, but time was suddenly heavy on his heart. He didn't feel young again, as he had imagined he somehow would. He was thirty-six, and he knew that he was not too old for a new beginning, in spite of five years wasted in the war. Yet he felt his back against the wall, and his anxiety was unalleviated. He had more time for his poetry, but he couldn't find a poetic phrase in his head. He began to send out some of his old poems, feeling it was time he tried to publish something, but they came back one by one, rejected. He finished off Ida's cigarettes and bought himself a bottle of Jim Beam. When these were gone Harry bought another carton, and another bottle.

He needed, he knew, a good job in order to meet his obligations and maintain himself. He wanted to be able to send his mother a check once in a while, too. He knew he was all washed up as far as security clearances went, and his only other thought was for the business world. Harry didn't relish the idea, but there wasn't any line of work that really appealed to him. He wrote to as many college textbook publishers as he could think of and finally landed a job with a big company as their Midwest representative. It didn't pay as much as he had hoped, but he thought he would manage if he stayed in the second best motels and saved some of his expense money. He rented a small furnished room for himself in Kansas City. It was an old building inhabited by elderly people, but he didn't mind because the rates were cheap.

Harry had one more brief affair and almost a second on his new job. He was in line by himself in a Kansas City cafeteria when he heard someone behind him calling his name. It was one of his former students from Montana, a girl with memorable thighs who had sat with precariously short skirts in the first row of his class. They had lunch together, and she explained that she had never finished college and was working as a beautician. Harry wasn't surprised. When he told her he was divorced she volunteered her phone number.

The first time Harry called her they spent the night in his room—she had two girlfriends sharing her apartment—and the following day Harry was served an eviction notice by his landlord. He changed his mind about old people for neighbors, and he began to wonder about his singular lack of discretion when it came to lovemaking. He took another place nearby, but in the end it turned out to be more than he could afford, and he had to move again. He missed the peace and quiet of his first room, and only then did he realize how well the place for old folks had suited him.

Harry never saw his former student again. He called her

again one winter night after he had been to a cheap theater that showed burlesque films, but one of her roommates answered and told him she had married.

Harry had a chance for a second affair with a young woman who was an English instructor at the university in Columbia, Missouri. It was early March on a Friday afternoon, Harry's favorite time of the week, and he was in her office trying to interest her in a textbook. He looked up and noticed that she seemed more interested in him. She had taken off her glasses and was smiling at him. Harry was suddenly aware that she was an attractive woman, but she looked sensitive and intelligent and maybe a little too slender for him. He decided she was not his kind, not at the moment, anyway.

"Well," Harry said, "I have to make St. Louis tonight. I thank you for your time."

It was a lie, of course, and she put on her glasses and stopped smiling.

Later, walking up the strollway and looking in the shop windows, Harry wished that he had at least asked her to dinner. It was twilight, and he felt lonely. On the second floor of his hotel he could see men and women embracing behind drawn shades. It looked for a moment like a Roman orgy, but then everyone suddenly changed partners and he remembered the dance studio which operated there at odd hours.

Starlings were clustered on the building ledges, making a tremendous racket as the sun went down. The still luminous sky southwest of the earth silhouetted the black branches of oaks and elms that loomed on the horizon of the city like a network of roots by which the planet clung to the universe. It reminded Harry vaguely of a sky he had witnessed several times early in the war: burning London after the Germans had bombed it. He thought of the girl he had picked up in Soho, and he wished he were not going to be alone that night.

The following September Harry was forced to go to a finance company to meet his obligations to Ida. He tried to adjust

to rooms that were worse than second rate, but he found them
too depressing. In one, in a Wichita motel where an exposed
light bulb hung down from the ceiling on a cord, he smelled
flesh in the bathroom. Later, taking a bath, he discovered on the
edge of the tub several large callouses—pared from the feet, perhaps, of some solitary traveler like himself.

He was passing through Columbia on a Friday night, and
on Saturday morning he strolled about the campus, hoping
vaguely to see again the woman who had smiled at him. The
campus was quiet, and as he walked Harry felt an emotion he
couldn't name. Turning the corner, he thought the woman who
came into view on the walk ahead of him might be the one he
half-heartedly sought.

He presumed she was on her way home, but before she left
the campus she entered a building that looked only recently
completed. Harry followed cautiously, with curiosity and longing, thinking he ought to be framing an alibi in case he should
come suddenly upon her, yet unable to do so. Within the building there was the smell of fresh paint and plaster, but no living
being, as far as he could determine. Then he heard a noise, a
door closing, echoing from a far stairwell. Pursuing it, he looked
with surprise down the winding metal stairs which must have
descended several stories below the ground. He hesitated before
plunging into what his imagination kept suggesting was some secret tunnel he had discovered to the bowels of the earth. For an
instant, Harry was struck by the incongruity, the implausibility
of his situation, as if at that moment he were removed from and
observing himself. He felt unalterably alone then, his longing
overcoming his uneasiness, and he descended the stairs in search
of the noise he had heard, of which some person, he reasoned,
must surely have been the source.

At first he saw no one. The stairway ran into a closed door,
and, opening it, Harry thought he had reached a cul de sac. He
stood before a dimly lighted room of bulky shadows which he
recognized were cast by boiler room equipment. He was about

to retrace his steps when he was arrested by another noise, a sharp metallic clinking. Something moved in the dim room and emerged between amorphous pieces of dark machinery. He was confronted by a white-haired, trembling figure: a wrinkled, mole-like old man in gray janitorial attire, leaning on a mop. Harry felt the squinting eyes fasten upon him inquisitively.

In his room that evening, alone with his bourbon, Harry put *Ride of the Valkyrie* on his portable hi-fi and watched that magnificent race of warrior women, long of limb and golden-haired, pass through the darkness of his room. Then he began to wonder what the woman at the university had seen in him in the first place. He had noticed that his hair had begun to thin. His eyes were usually bloodshot, and he thought his nostrils seemed slightly enlarged from his nervous habit of fingering them.

"I could never afford her," he said aloud to himself in a voice that was strangely hoarse. He hated himself for having once preferred the beautician, his former student, to this young woman.

He dreamed that night again of the blonde of his college days whom he had loved. In the dream, she was as tall as Harry. They met at a party, in a room full of people, and later, leaving together, she pressed close to Harry and told him she had never been able to forget him.

Harry awoke unnerved by the fact that she should still occur in his dreams. Thinking how he had lied and failed and wasted life, and remembering how abruptly his romance with her had ended, he thought now that he could understand why.

"Can it be," he asked himself, "that she knew me better than I knew myself?"

Later that fall things went from bad to worse for Harry. He didn't keep to his traveling schedule for his company. He went anxiously to his burlesque films and he spent long hours in newsstands looking at girlie magazines. And he kept buying the Jim Beam.

He was staying at a motel in Joplin when he came down with the flu—he hadn't been taking care of himself. For days he just lay in bed with his bottle and a fever. He checked in with his company two weeks behind schedule and found himself dismissed. He was told the company hadn't been satisfied with him anyway.

It occurred to Harry that all he had in the world were his clothes, his portable hi-fi, and his books. With a kind of perverse and defiant logic he gave all his clothes, except an old army trenchcoat and the ones he was wearing, to the Salvation Army. He donated the phonograph and all his books, except Henry David Thoreau's *Walden*, to the nearest library. He notified his landlord that he would be out the following day. Then he went to a burlesque theater and saw a marvelous big stripper whose flaming red hair hung down to the small of her back.

"You marvelous big thing," Harry sighed to himself after he had begun to drink in his room. His mind wallowed freely in his lust, and he was tormented by a desire to relieve himself. He tried to think of something else he wanted to do.

Harry started to read Henry David Thoreau's *Walden*. He read the last chapter first, and he lingered on the part where Thoreau described the butterfly coming out of the farmer's applewood table, like some kind of resurrection. Harry wondered whether Henry David Thoreau meant to imply a resurrection, and whether he could be resurrected himself. He didn't believe in immortality. He surmised that Thoreau must have been talking about a man's potential in this life, and thinking about his own life, Harry saw how he had succumbed to shameful sensuality. It was no good, he knew, blaming it all on his anxiety. He decided then upon a pilgrimage. He would hitchhike to Walden Pond and spend the rest of the winter there, where Thoreau had lived a century before.

But then Harry read the introduction to *Walden* by a scholar in his own century, and when he finished he was sorry he had read it. The scholar explained that Thoreau's pond had been made into a public beach and that authorities had found that among the waters of the greater Boston area the pond ranked high in urine content. Moreover, he advanced the Freudian theory that Thoreau's practice of immersing himself in Walden Pond was a manifestation of his suppressed sensuality.

Harry decided not to go to Walden Pond after all. He remembered how blue the water had looked when he had last passed by the Lake of the Ozarks, and he decided to go there instead. Blue was Harry's favorite color.

Ida told the investigator that she didn't know whether Harry could swim or not. She had never seen him try. The investigator explained that a copy of *Walden* with Harry's name in it had been found in the boat drifting near the middle of the lake. It was a big lake and they might never find the body, he said. It had happened before.

Harry's body was never found in the lake, but it couldn't be located anywhere else, either. Ida's child support stopped coming, of course, but her father had died in a forgiving mood and she had inherited all she needed for herself and Elaine. She couldn't blame herself for what had happened to Harry; she remembered, in fact, that he had once praised her for having the patience of a saint. Still, she couldn't help feeling uncomfortable about Harry and that drifting boat.

She told Elaine that Harry had been a good but unfortunate man, and she believed this to be true. But she taught her she should never, never put her trust in love. Harry had always feared she might teach her something like that.

Summerfield

*L*IFE WOULD BE EASY IF WE HAD ONLY TO LIVE IT. MY FRIEND Summerfield once asked me what I meant by that, but we were having a reunion dinner in Juarez at the time and the champagne had gone to our heads, so I never had to explain.

We had grown up together in a little town in New Mexico. I no longer had any attachments there—my parents had long since left the region—but after the war I found myself longing for the bright sunlight and an indefinable warmth that I traced to my boyhood years with Summerfield. I sought him first of all my friends after the war, needing the unclouded blue eyes and the shy friendliness I had known so well. Yet I sought in vain, and standing one evening before the house he had lived in I thought how close we had been. As boys we wrestled together on the hard loam of the schoolgrounds. Sometimes I won, but sometimes he pinned my shoulders to the frozen ground, and for the life of me I could not throw him over. Born on the same day, of the same height and slender build, we had sometimes passed for twins, though I had always to acknowledge to myself with a pang of envy that I found something keen and wonderfully perceptive in his character, betrayed by his every gesture, which I could not find in myself.

It was not surprising he was gone. New houses were everywhere, and smoke from a lumber mill muddied the sky. Everything about the town was changing. Some years later I learned that Summerfield too had been lured back to it and met by a disappointment similar to my own.

I had by then married the girl we had both once been partial to—though there was never any rivalry between us—and gone off to Southwest City to teach in a high school, the profession of my father and the one I had prepared for before the war. It was in the fall of my second year of teaching, when I was attending a convention in El Paso, that I saw him. The circumstances of our meeting and the evening that followed seem almost unreal to me even now.

It was late on a Saturday afternoon and the convention had ended. Everyone I knew had checked out of the hotel and gone to the airport, but my own plane did not leave until Sunday morning. I pondered what to do with myself and settled into a chair in the hotel lobby. I thought of a bum on the street who had wanted to make North Carolina, of old men sitting alone in the cafeteria where I had lunched, of the well-dressed man and his wife in the bookstore where I had browsed who made cynical jokes about the president. Three elderly people sitting near me were striking up a conversation about nothing. The lady had laughed at one of the men when he came in wearing the other man's hat.

I got up and went to the hotel bar, looking for convention stragglers like myself. Above the bar a television set was tuned to a late-season football game, and a few men in business suits lounged about watching half-heartedly. People are bored with football, I thought. Even the announcer's voice could tell you this.

Saturday afternoon and depression. I wished then that I had asked the bum from North Carolina to dinner. I went back to my chair in the lobby and watched a group of men standing nearby talking—not polished and not businessmen either; ranchers, perhaps. One said in a raised voice, "Glad to have you aboard, Tom," and then they broke up and departed in all directions. In their wake, in that moment, crossing the lobby toward me with top coat in arm and suitcase in hand, emerged a figure I recognized at once as Summerfield. No one had been further from my thoughts at that time, but I would have known that youthful brightness anywhere.

He stopped when he saw me, setting down his luggage deliberately. I got up, and then we met midway, shaking hands, and I found myself looking again into the tanned face and the clear eyes.

Yet he was different, and though I have tried to explain it to myself I can't say how. Perhaps the eyes were not as untroubled as I remembered them, perhaps the mouth seemed drawn, or perhaps it was the hair, less fair, retreating vaguely from the forehead. Still, he wore a blue dress shirt and a tweed coat that were becoming to him, and I had to remind myself that he was, after all, as old as I was. In answer to my inquiries he told me—somewhat apologetically, I thought—that he was traveling for a New York publishing house. I was disappointed. I had expected something nobler of him.

An hour later we were crossing the bridge to Juarez in the autumn twilight. I seemed to recall that it was not the first time we had done this, though I had forgotten or never noticed the way the neon fury of that border city ignited the haze that hung over the river, and how the Rio Grande, feeble and distracted at that point in its course, was barely audible in the din of the young evening. It was Saturday and one saw American servicemen in every block. Proprietors of the little sidewalk shops accosted the tourists, and cab drivers on every corner were touting for the brothels. At one corner a man with both legs amputated was selling flowers, scooting about laboriously on a wooden plank mounted on roller skate wheels. "*Flores*," he called. "*Flores para su novia.*"

We shouldered our way into a restaurant, and over dinner

he spoke mournfully of his separation from his wife and daughter. "It's hard when you're on the road," Summerfield complained, and then he warned, with sudden solemnity, "Stay off the road if you can help it." I had the inspiration to order champagne, which turned out to be a bad mistake. Our conversation took a metaphysical turn, and we spoke thickly for awhile of the good life and lamented the defacement of San Anselmo, our home town, and then, all judgment gone, we ordered more. I can't remember who suggested it, or whether we just mutely arrived at the same idea, but sometime after that we were in a taxi headed for a brothel. I was betraying my bad Spanish to the driver, and while he humored us, I was aware enough to know that he was hating us all the while.

We crossed the bridge again after midnight, and down on the sand bars of the dark river below us, barefoot and ragged, three Mexican boys were begging pennies. It will seem incongruous, but my moral sense began to stir, for I had never been able to cross over that bridge with an easy conscience. To toss them pennies as they expected seemed haughty, but to give them a dollar only intensified the problem: why not more? Everything? Yet to give them nothing, to ignore them, seemed worst of all. I watched Summerfield.

He paused at the railing, pressed up close to it, and looked down contemptuously. It was some moments before I realized what he was doing, and when I did I could not believe it. That he should be capable of such an act escaped my understanding. No, this was not the boy I had known. We did not need to understand the outburst of invective from below us, and there was such health and fury in it that I later wondered whether there had not been some obscure compassion behind Summerfield's gesture after all.

We said goodbye in the hotel lobby. We were sober and sleepy by then, and he seemed sullen and depressed. Until that night I had never imagined him capable of such demeanor. When we shook hands he looked at me for an instant with accusation in his face, and I noticed that his eyes were bloodshot.

That evening later seemed a bad dream. When I wrote to him once at the address he had given me and got no reply, I thought perhaps it had been. And yet after the encounter everything about me changed almost imperceptibly. I was homesick for a town and a boyhood friend who no longer existed, and my wife concluded that my constant references to my past betrayed my present unhappiness. All of this confounded me, and added to it I found myself disillusioned with my vocation, the vocation of my father before me. That summer we made the first of a series of restless moves, dragging our newly born son with us. We moved to Nevada hoping for a new start.

There were things about the Nevada desert that reminded me of home, yet it was not home, and I had the terrible sensation that I would never find whatever it was I sought. A year went by and we moved again, this time to a California town at the end of the continent. It was an idyllic setting. No one could have asked for more. And yes, for awhile we were happy, that summer in a rented house that overlooked the sea. But school started, and by late summer the fog was rolling in on us regularly, and to me the whole earth turned foreign.

My disenchantment with my work persisted. It was as if I had nothing to teach, and when I spoke before the class I heard the sound of my own voice.

One day when summer had just come round again I was crossing the highway that ran through the town. The first warmth of the season was reflecting from it, and something about the road and the hot breath of life made me think of smaller towns further inland, burnt-over crossroads in the desert I had passed through in the sundowns of summer. I had an illusion of freedom such as I imagine hoboes have. I thought of the railroad towns with the names that were magic to me, Rock Island, Ash Fork,

Laramie. Summer and life, and for an instant I felt I had forever with my life.

Since then I see the enormity of the lie that conspired against me, but in that moment I felt I had forever. I crossed a highway, and in that moment, almost unaware, I made my decision. I gave up everything and threw away my life.

I had no desire to be anything but a wayfarer, a passerby over the alien earth. I remembered Summerfield and wrote to the company in New York that he traveled for. I was informed that he was no longer with them, but my application was invited. I was hired, and thus it was I found myself about to do what I had thought poorly of my old friend for doing, and I wanted to see him again now that I understood. I was sent to New York for a week of training, and on my last night there I believe I had a glimpse of him.

I spent my free hours walking the sidewalks of the Village, which teemed with people on the August night. A wonderful sense of tolerance was present, such as one refugee might extend to another. I could not help thinking that I was certain to know someone out of the millions of people in the city I walked, and on my last night, crossing a street a block below Washington Square, I almost bumped into him—I'm sure it was he, Summerfield, walking with a woman who did not meet the description of the wife he had spoken of in Juarez. I called after him and, momentarily, he turned. There were people between us by then, but I recognized his face, although I was surprised at the look of dissipation I found there. He turned again when he saw me and continued on his way. He did not want to know me. I was just as glad, and I could understand, for I had learned by then to relish the freedom of my loneliness.

How shall I describe the subtle changes which took place in me during my first year of traveling? I no longer had to stand before a class and listen to my own voice, and I sank into silence willingly. It was as if a great weight had been lifted from me.

"Something is happening," my wife warned. I had all of Arizona and part of California to travel, but even at home I was distant and removed. Again thereafter she would say, "I don't like what's happening to you." I listened silently, knowing I could not explain, nor could she. It was indefinable.

Finally she accused me, perhaps rightly in her way, of being unfaithful. I had not been, unless you consider the peculiar faithlessness of a distracted man. Eventually she left me, taking our young son with her. Separation was what I seemed to want, she contended. I was barely aware of the pleasure I took in my aloneness. It was inevitable that it should be complete.

Some months after our separation something happened to me which I do not yet fully comprehend, a very simple but singular event, which I now believe changed the course of my life again.

I was visiting with my son, and we had gone to the beach at San Clemente. It was a Saturday afternoon in late October, near the end of the beach season. The sun was dropping, the tide rising. I held my son's hand as we waded out of the surf, the sun low at our backs, and I looked down and saw our shadows in the swirling water, my own long shadow beside that of the small boy. That was all. It was just an image: two shadows in the surf at sundown. But it was everything, and the image haunted me.

I had a long drive to Flagstaff ahead of me the next morning, and as I drove east into the desert I could feel that something was wrong. I did not know what. Something had crept into the edge of my self-possession and would not leave me.

I had reached Indio and was attempting to banish my uneasiness, and there just beyond the cutoff to Blythe the first hitchhiker appeared, a boy with a wholesome face, a white shirt and tie and a black book which must have been a Bible. Then another, a black man in a baseball cap who inclined his head toward the car suggestively, and finally another, standing beside the road where it curved to climb up through the sandhills above the valley. As I passed I saw the man throw something—it looked like a bottle—across the road in disgust because I would not stop. I looked closely at the faces whenever I passed them, drawn to them magnetically, and again in my mirror, expecting to see them curse me.

I made Blythe by noon and crossed the Colorado River into Arizona. The sky was clear and the desert was heating up. A flight of birds flushed at the roadside, and I winged one of them. Looking back in the mirror I saw it raise its good wing from the pavement the way I imagined a drowning man would clutch at the air. I wondered how much consciousness a bird possessed, how much light behind the eyes was turning dark and murky.

Then at midafternoon my fanbelt snapped, and I slowed down carefully and limped ten miles into the next town, the little village of Aguila, and pulled into the first service station. A Mexican boy came out to wait on me. Yes, they had a mechanic, and he went to rouse him from a small and weatherbeaten house trailer parked in the lot beside the station. He came back directly to say it would be a few minutes. As I waited I wondered what it was that drove a man to live in such an unlikely place, a tradesman with a skill who might have lived elsewhere. And did he live alone? Yes, surely he was alone, and surely he was in some kind of exile, in penance, perhaps. I pondered the concept of penance. I do not know why it came to mind.

It was a leafless, sun-baked village, but the breeze stirring in the colored pennants strung above the station attracted my attention. When I looked down again a man in dirty coveralls had emerged from the trailer and was walking toward me. All the uneasiness that had plagued me that day raced up my spine. I knew him at once, in spite of all aging, and I think he knew me too, for he hesitated momentarily and then came forward with his face averted.

He raised the hood and worked behind it as behind a shield, but when he finished and brought it down he gave me a momentary glance, calm and direct, which pierced me like a scream. Then without a word he turned abruptly toward his trailer.

The boy came out again and I paid him. I drove out onto the highway half-stupefied, searching for the word that would name what I had seen in the face of Summerfield. For somewhere there was a word I had forgotten or repressed which would name it, and when I finally found it I knew it was the name for all the vague emotions that had haunted me since I had seen my shadow in the surf. And the word was guilt.

Giant saguaro began to beckon. They held out thumbs and they accosted like hitchhikers and cab drivers I thought I had forgotten. It was my guilt they played upon. They appealed like wife and child, or like father or Summerfield they stood accusing. Only the gathering dusk spared me their faces, faces I feared I would meet again in hell, as if forgiving were beyond the nature of things.

I climbed up the first mountain in the ascent toward Flagstaff. At Peeple's Valley I watched the birds rise slowly from the fields into the October sky. A jet trail hung there in the haze.

Beyond Prescott there is another valley, a great incredible expanse of high plateau which the thin highway crosses on its way to Mingus mountain. If you happen to hit that stretch of the road alone at late afternoon, as I have, drive slowly, look perhaps into the eye of the steer that's standing by the roadside, and tell me what you feel. If you say you cannot, then I'll confide I've known the feeling.

But now there was a car ahead of me, a single car with a man and a woman sitting close together, and as I drew closer I saw a child, a small boy, standing in the seat between them. They drove slowly and stared toward Mingus Mountain, and suddenly I was moved by what I saw, by the beholders themselves, by the boy, fairhaired and beloved, who was Summerfield, who was me in my childhood, who stared out and did not know yet what I knew, and who would know only when it was too late to know.

At a little hill blurred with the green of pine and the red of dying oak I pulled the car to the side of the road. I could smell the pines and see the sunlight catching the hilltop. I was going to climb toward it. I was going to climb to it, and I was going to whisper to the sky where it lived, "Summerfield, Summerfield." After that, in the dark, I did not know what I would do, and it did not matter.

No, that was not the end of me. We say we throw our lives away, and yet we go on living. I mended mine as best I could, and managed to reconcile with my wife. I gave up the road and took a job writing reports for an engineering concern in South-west City, that sprawling metropolis where we had started out.

What else was one to do? I reconciled myself, and did what I should have done no doubt in the first place. In time, perhaps, I'll call it home.

We'd taken to driving in the suburbs on the weekends, looking over the new houses which all looked alike, in quest of our new home, and one Sunday afternoon I saw a distracted-looking man out walking his dog, a man who looked vaguely familiar.

Yes, that was the last time I saw him. He was standing there on the corner holding the dog on the leash. We waved, and I honked the horn. We did not stop. In the mirror I saw him raise his hand and wave, and then looking after us, somewhat bewildered, he crossed the street with the dog. I believe he rec-ognized us at the last instant, but then you can't be sure about a thing like that.

A mutual friend tells me he lives with his aging mother, that he has found a place for himself at last with the university, but I divine that if you could look down on him some evening as he makes his way home through the shadows of that shapeless city, you might see him pounding his breast or tearing his hair. It is the same with him: he is restless and changing still. And in this he will never change.

The Changes

*F*EELING HIMSELF DRIFTING, HE LOOKED AND SAW THE TRAIN was laboring slowly through an immense and grimy industrial area: bleak warehouses and motor pools crowded with trucks, blackened brick buildings with little smoke-stained windows where people not unlike his father had worked their lives away, and then, at first sandwiched between buildings and then shoulder to shoulder for block on block, the houses of the poor, feeble frame dwellings left unpainted and uncared for in their old age.

He brushed his hand across his face. Putting the gray city behind him, he tried to see into the country ahead and recalled, buoyantly, the expanding high plains of Kansas and Colorado, little towns signaled by groves that gathered around elevated grain and water towers, solitary farm houses and windmills, alone among vast expanses of sky and rolling earth, and further, dimly remembered, the high mountains. On his flight east he had glimpsed them in the distance, and now they were his reason for returning on this quietly gliding train.

He remembered the long journey there when he was just a boy and his mother and father were not yet old—his father had loved that passage west. They had driven slowly and peered in silence. They had been happy then, perhaps closer together at that time of his life than they had ever been since. He began to doze, but not before another image had crossed his mind, an image in which he journeyed happily with his wife across a wide and white winter landscape, while bundled warmly on the car seat between them lay his own infant son. Catching each other's glance, the mother and father had smiled.

Some hours later he woke in the hurtling dark and caught the glint of a stream wandering feebly in the desolate starlight.

"What river is that?" he asked the passing form of the conductor.

"*Huerfano,*" he heard, and then, as he continued to stare at the disembodied whisper, "the orphan."

In the dawn, he stood rubbing his eyes in the little town of San Anselmo, watching the train, with its sprinkling of weary passengers, toil further into the mountains en route to the end of the continent. When it was out of sight he looked a long moment the other way, down the tracks. From the green fields beyond the tracks burst the song of a meadowlark. Behind him somewhere in the town there was also the sound of water, the sound of mountain water finding its way over stone. There was not another sound. He stood there alone.

Then he began to walk. In the darkness he had ascended this green and flowering mountain, and now he wanted to walk in the dawn, in the calm. He wanted to walk in the song of a bird and the sound of water and stones. He had no memory for anything else. There were houses and shops and churches and a lumber mill, but he had no memory for them. There was only the calm and the light and the feeling of green fields, the song and the sound of water and stones.

He stood on the wooden bridge watching the mountain

stream in its borders of willow and box elder. He followed a path along it and came to a bench under an old cottonwood. He sat and surveyed the grass of a little green park. At the far end there were two deserted tennis courts, with worn nets and sagging fences. They seemed visited only by the host of hollyhocks that stood in a burst of color against the near fence, gazing silently.

His hand passed over his eyes and he closed them. There was the sound of falling water behind him, and he could remember only the meadowlark, the bird with the yellow breast which he had not seen but had known like a friend, spilling its heart out in the joy of its song.

Presently he opened his eyes to the discord of a passing bumblebee, and he saw, surprisingly, that two players had taken to one of the tennis courts. They were a father and his small son, it seemed, the father floating the ball toward the boy almost tenderly, the boy laughing for joy, both of them occasionally speaking, he thought, although from where he watched he could not hear them. They did not intrude upon his solitude. Hypnotically, he followed the soundless white sphere cleaving the morning light as it crossed the ancient net between them.

He was distracted again by the chaotic rasping of the bumblebee, but it vanished as quickly as it had appeared, and in its wake there came a peal of sound that seemed to fall across the park like the sudden shadow of a cloud before the sun, darkening his mood, bringing back memory. Indeed, the tennis players ceased their play and looked up at the sky as if they had forgotten something. They gathered their belongings and left the park amid the tolling of the solemn bells. He had forgotten it was Sunday morning.

Retracing his path along the stream, he remembered a park in a faraway time. As they bent to gather all the tennis balls they had beat across the net between them, he saw his father shiver in the falling sun.

Getting off his bus in Southwest City he scanned the faces

in the depot, hoping to spot his wife. He went inside and tele-phoned, but hung up, gently, while it was ringing.

Outside again with his luggage, he climbed into a cab and rolled the window down. The desert air was warm and not un-pleasant, and the lights of the traffic moved calmly along the avenue like a slow stream. If he had waited for them to answer, he thought, his son might have come to pick him up, and they would have driven home with nothing to say to each other. He was glad to be riding alone, but he missed the sweet fragrance of the mountain town, and in the rumble of the traffic there was no sound of mountain water.

A yellow convertible full of gazing teenagers pulled up to perch beside the cab at a red light. When the light turned green, one of them yelled something unintelligible, and the car screeched away amid a burst of laughter.

When he turned from the cab with his bags in hand he saw her standing there in the doorway.

"Did you call?" Her voice drifted across the lawn to him. "Someone called and then hung up." His son had come to the door now too and seemed to be regarding him intently—a little contemptuously, he thought.

He was about to say no, but he checked himself.

"Yes," he said. "I called and then hung up."

He saw them exchange glances, then he looked away. He felt her gaze on him, not hostile, but he would have never known her as a friend, either.

He had gotten just the right touch of irony into his voice, he thought.

On Monday he was back to work where people in the office offered condolences about his father, but at home she sometimes remarked how he had changed. It was true that he had quit read-ing the newspapers, and once he confessed he'd been forming sympathies for the people on "wanted" notices in the post office.

"Have you ever considered," he asked her abruptly one evening, "the ugliness of human eyelashes? Ugly fur-lined orifices are what our eyes are."

She stared awhile, then moved quietly to retire. He was feeling rather hollow, but carried on compulsively.

"Or take the ugliness of ears," he announced. "Surely they are like nothing human, considered by themselves. A woman does damn well to cover them behind her hair."

"God, how you've changed," she was saying, staring blankly.

And he, thinking of his father, of his son, passing his hand across his face, said ever so sincerely, "Haven't we all?"

Enemies in the City

ABOUT SUMMERFIELD I SHALL NEVER CEASE TO SPECULATE. No, as I've confided already, I never saw him again after our last encounter, but there remains an interval thereafter when I lived with a sense of his presence—a kind of empathy that enabled me on occasion to divine his very consciousness. And, on such occasions, what I divined above all was his forlorn dejection, a bitter and acute melancholy, with the exception that where I was concerned—it saddens me to say it—there was a certain inimical curiosity about my affairs which approached malevolence.

It must have been some inkling of this last sentiment that prevented me from befriending him, from going round to look him up now that I knew we were once again living in the same city. Even so I sometimes found myself on the threshold of doing just that, for I have only lately stumbled against one of life's finer consolations. I refer, of course, to what men call friendship, that balm for all aging and despair, the deprivation of which has

surely proven one of the sorest consequences of the nomadic existence we've both pursued.

I have yet to account to myself for my discovery—which
strikes me as rather like a blind man discovering color—except
to say that my mind now pauses frequently on those long ago
days I took too much for granted, when we, Summerfield and I,
were constant companions. For my son has left home now, and
my wife has gone silent. Of a Sunday I walk, in the park, in the
streets, I walk and I watch, and coming home in the twilight to
a dark house I am met with these silences. Then one evening I
am amazed:

"You had a visitor," she says with her back to me.

Dumbfounded, I ask "Who?"

"A visitor," she repeats.

"Who?"

"A Mr. Shelley." And saying this, she turns around, smiling
like a sybil. "He's been hanging around for days. I've decided to
keep him. I gave him a bath in the kitchen sink and he did this
to me."

She holds up her hand and shows me where her wrist has
been bitten, and to my mind there rises, finally, an image of the
sullen, brindled tomcat, mauled and half-starved, who has appeared from nowhere at our kitchen door and refuses to vanish.

"I've decided to keep him. He's so sad, so forlorn. I need
someone."

That night we were both awakened by the telephone ringing. There was no one there—or rather, there was someone
there, I sensed, but whoever it was was silent. In such cases I
remain silent myself and I listen. After awhile I heard someone
exhale, and then the disconnection.

She stared at me, and then smiled.

"I *said* you had a visitor."

She held up her hand again and showed me where the wrist
was bitten.

"He did this to me when I scrubbed him and ran up the curtain."

I stared dumbfounded.

"You're rabid," I said.

That night I sat up alone and watched the Night Owl Movie, a Humphrey Bogart film called *High Sierra*. There were scenes filmed near the village of Independence where we'd spent a weekend years ago in our wanderings.

It had been a weekend in October, and the whole Owens Valley in the forgotten back side of California was quiet and cool and tranquil. We drove up the valley and into the foothills to a place called Convict Lake, deserted then and shining in the high brilliant light. All around the grass had turned golden, and below the lake a clear brook ran undisturbed down the great sloping fields of golden turf on the mountainside.

We slept that night in the village, in the cold darkness which came early behind the mountain. We had lived a day in the light and the darkness, and I remember wishing that the cycle could go on forever, that we could live in a house in that village, like the house Mary Austin had lived in, and throw our clocks away.

In the end, as I recall, they hunted Bogart out of his mountain hideout and killed him.

There was blood on the kitchen steps. Mr. Shelley had come back. He was at the kitchen door that morning, looking up at my wife, at her eyes, when she went out to sit on the garden bench beside the iris in bloom. She'd called the animal shelter where he was being held for observation, and the man had confessed, with obvious embarrassment, that he'd gotten away from them. I resolved to take him back at the earliest opportunity. But that morning, seeing my silent wife beside the blue iris, I lingered in the yard with her, as if enchanted. It was a fine spring morning, and I remember Mr. Shelley, basking in the sun beside the kitchen steps, exerting himself momentarily to swat at a passing butterfly.

She sat there looking soft and pensive. She wore a pale blue house dress, her wrist was bandaged, and she looking lovely as the blue iris beside her. She would not quite consent to look at me or speak to me, and sitting there beside her in that Elysian light my heart suddenly ached for the beauty of her and the won-der of that soft disdain.

So this is what it has come to, I thought.

She sat there mute while I, to my own wonder, began to speak in a torrent. . . .

It was for me a discovery which rivaled, say, the discovery of a continent. If that exquisite ache were love, I'd never loved her as I did at that moment, and I remember that I told her so, among my many words, though whether she heard me or not I'll never know. I remember, too, thinking later that in the life of every man there must come such moments, but precious few.

That day at the office my sense of Elysium dissolved into uneasiness. Near two o'clock I was called to the telephone. I an-swered twice, and then my heart stood still at the heavy silence attending me. I held my breath and listened. It seemed like min-utes that passed, and then, just before the hum, a long exhala-tion, the expiration of the faintest sigh.

By three I called an ambulance and excused myself, ex-plaining, belatedly, that I'd had an emergency at home.

There were neighbors at their windows, staring, when I ar-rived. The ambulance had come and gone. And there was blood on the steps again.

At the hospital I am allowed only a brief visit. She is very pale, like the time I first saw her after our son was born, and both wrists are bandaged. And she is silent.

I talk, trying to summon the mood of the morning. "Do you remember the time we went to Convict Lake?" I ask. "It was

October and the tourists had all gone home. Everything was beautiful. And cold. There was a beautiful cold that brought tears to your eyes. You kept saying how cold you were. We walked around the village that night and a wind came up, a little wind in the clear night and the stars, and your teeth began to chatter. That night in bed. . . ."

Whatever it is, she doesn't want me to talk. "We could go there again," I offer. "We could go there again and throw away our clocks." I try to explain that it's an old Humphrey Bogart movie on the late show that's made me think of it, but she doesn't seem to hear.

The next morning the wind had still been stirring, animating the dead leaves on the ground, and in the blue-brilliant sky there had been the cry of migrating geese.

The next night I am denied a visit. I am met instead by a doctor who says he's had a long talk with her. He advises a period of separation. It's her request, too, he says, which I should honor if I want what's best for her. She'll be all right, but they will want to keep her awhile, in another place, for observation. In a place, I suppose, that they have for such cases.

So this is what it has come to.

I'm alone in the house now, and one night, late, the phone rings. I lift the receiver carefully and, without speaking, hear the ticking of a clock.

I remember, too, a day, a Sunday, a fog-bound afternoon when I was alone in the house we had rented on the coast of California. The phone rang, and I heard, through the fog, the voice of my father—he seemed a light-year away. Alone, he wanted to talk.

"I thought I'd tell you, Son, if I ever told anybody. I knew you'd understand."

Was there anything wrong, I started to ask, but checked myself.

51

"It's just. . . ." There was a pause, and then I knew he'd changed his mind.

All the same, the dark was removed from my eyes. For a moment—no, for days—I began to see.

I shall probably take to retiring early, even if I sleep restlessly, and rising at dawn. I shall hate to miss the light.

In the restaurants where I used to eat I am ignored by the waitresses, and the neighbors, seeing me come and go, still come to their windows to stare. I'll probably move again, and we'll both go on living, closer to home as the clock counts.

Someone is behind it all, I can't help thinking. Someone innocent of compassion but insatiably curious, eavesdropping. The tabby cat, Mr. Shelley, was found not to be rabid, and yet I never went back to pick him up. I don't know what became of him, but may have seen him crossing my path a time or two.

"I need someone," she had said, and I realize now, thinking of that abandoned cat she had so desperately tried to befriend, that this was terribly true: desperately, she needed someone.

I have this haunting fear that I am no one.

Beauty and the Beast

D R. SHELLEY WAS ELAINE SUMMERFIELD'S FIRST ACQUAINT-
ance on the faculty at the university in Southwest City.
She met him the day she registered. She came late and fearful
that he, as her advisor, would be out of patience with her for not
coming the day before, which was set aside exclusively for entering freshmen. As she wandered uncertainly in the heat and confusion of the crowded gymnasium, she sensed that registration
day in itself was enough to exhaust the patience of even the
most phlegmatic professor.

She finally located the English section toward the middle of
a long row of tables which extended across the west wall of the
gymnasium, where the noise seemed to subside slightly. She surveyed the grave-looking men corraled between the wall and the
tables, and, quite by chance, Dr. Shelley was the first whom she
approached. She introduced herself and was slightly surprised
when he exclaimed, a little hoarsely, she thought, "Ah yes, then
I'm your advisor." She was about to offer her excuse for her ab-

sence the preceding day when she heard him say again, cheerfully, "Ah yes, we missed you yesterday." Elaine detected the hoarseness in his voice again, and this time she thought that emotion, as well as fatigue, was the source of it. But the notion made her uneasy, and she decided she was probably mistaken.

Dr. Shelley wore gray gabardine pants and a faded corduroy coat. Elaine estimated that he was nearing fifty, if not already there. His brown hair had thinned noticeably and his six-foot frame was perhaps too lean, as if exhausted by an uncomfortable spirit. His voice remained pleasant, though a trifle hoarse, while he helped her arrange her schedule, and when she thanked him for everything and stood up to take her leave, he leaned back in his chair and smiled at her sincerely, but shyly—his eyes always seemed to avert from hers at the last moment. He is self-conscious because his eyes are bloodshot, Elaine thought. When, two hours later, she had completed all the processes of registration and was about to leave the gymnasium through the door marked "EXIT" by a large cardboard sign, she glanced back across the floor toward the English section and thought she saw Dr. Shelley following her with his eyes.

After a few weeks at the university Elaine thought she had made good choices in coming to the school and deciding to major in English. In both of these satisfactions she was aware of her debt to Dr. Shelley. Three times a week she attended his late afternoon class in English Composition in one of the oldest buildings on campus, a building which had been converted from a girls' dormitory. Dr. Shelley, whose office was in the same building, spoke of the rustle of nightgowns one still heard sometimes when working in the building late at night. Although all the buildings followed a uniform architectural pattern, she could detect the difference between the older buildings and the "new campus," as those imposing buildings that expanded toward and included her dormitory at the far end of the campus were collectively called.

The old campus sported most of the grass and trees, ancient elms and cottonwoods, and there was even a little pond with water lilies and a wooden bridge that she had to cross getting to Dr. Shelley's class. The newer buildings, though formidable, were more austere, and grass often gave way to more practical asphalt or cement.

"This nation of engineers will not be satisfied until the whole country is paved," Dr. Shelley remarked to his class one day as he glanced wistfully out the window at the autumn foliage.

In Dr. Shelley's classes Elaine received a kind of inspiration she had never known before. He asked unanswerable but provocative questions, contending it was shameful to go through college without examining one's values. Once, when they had read an essay about the remarkable intelligence of the porpoise, he began by asking what was the second most intelligent animal on earth. After receiving a variety of answers, he asked quietly, climactically, "Why not man?" For a moment he held the class in stunned silence. Then he launched into a series of unflattering images of man presented by contemporary writers, concluding with a passage of a poem which offered a kind of evolutionary view of original sin, in which the poet concluded he would rather be a worm in a wild apple than a son of man.

His class was outraged, but Dr. Shelley was not through. As the hour drew to a close and the winter dusk rose to the second-story windows, he changed the tone of his voice and observed that although man had the power to aid all living things he threatened the survival of even his own species. He confessed his sorrow at having accidentally run down a coyote on the highway one bleak winter night, "a beautiful wild creature like that," because some winter night man might have his back to the wall too, facing starvation like that coyote. A service station attendant had assured him it was good riddance, that the coyotes had been eating cattle, but Dr. Shelley concluded, with a sweeping gesture of humility, "So had I."

Usually at such moments the hour would end, and, momentarily spent, he would dismiss the class. At the next meeting, however, he surprisingly reversed his procedure and sat silent for half the period, his flushed face resting in his hands as if in contemplation. Then he left the class. Some of his students were amused, but Elaine found the experience strangely meaningful. She did not believe he was sufficiently appreciated. Most of his students, she observed, filed out of his classes with an air of indifference that she knew was painful to him. She could see he was truly dedicated, and she sometimes feared he would exhaust himself before the end of the semester.

But when the spring semester came she found herself in Dr. Shelley's class again, in the same room in the oldest building on campus. Although Dr. Shelley had posted only two F's among his final grades, Elaine saw none of her former classmates. She noticed that he retraced his way through some of the most passionate passages of his first semester lectures, but she still found herself enthralled, and he seemed grateful for her return.

She recognized in him a kindred spirit, for he made vivid a world which she flattered herself she had already dimly realized, full of countless evils, many of them hidden beneath the hypocrisy of the most hallowed American tradition. He called Billy the Kid a pimply-faced little murderer from Brooklyn and asked how many knew that Abe Lincoln used to frequent the brothels and take a keen delight in telling very dirty stories—he forgave Lincoln, saying that he only betrayed his humanity. He berated Americans generally, and when they were discussing an essay by Philip Wylie he maintained that America was a nation of "Mom" worshippers and described American mothers as overweight, middle-aged idols, with the intelligence of children, who had outlived their usefulness. This kind of cynicism Elaine came to understand as an instrument of provocation, for he was a passionate advocate of the Socratic "Examine all things" philosophy. Furthermore, was he not middle-aged himself, and was it not rumored that he lived with his aging mother? Elaine had seen him driving through the campus with her one Sunday in his little blue Volkswagen.

Elaine detected the despair of an idealist in his heart. "For all the evil in this world," he would say, "man is yet noble because he has a heart that can aspire," and in flights like these he was most admirable because he was most himself. He read romantic poetry with unashamed emotion, and although other students listened with what seemed a ruthless interest in Dr. Shelley and not the poetry, Elaine admired his sensitivity. He was reading an old ballad about a betrayed lover one day when he glanced at Elaine as he came to the last line. His cheeks drained white and he continued in a voice slightly hoarse, "For I am sick at the heart, and fain would lie doun." Stoically, without faltering, he recovered and went on. Elaine's eyes blurred. The purity of his spirit was overwhelming when such a mood possessed him.

For all his emotional display Dr. Shelley revealed his personal life but slightly. Elaine, finding herself intensely interested, learned all she could about him from her observations and from the various rumors which circulated about the campus. He did not seem to be popular, on the whole, with either his students or his colleagues. The latter might have been jealous, but she could not understand the apparent scorn of even the graduate students who she passed in the hall as they left his Romantic Poetry course.

He was a man of habit, a trait common to many professors, and one which consequently vaguely disappointed her. He dressed neatly but with monotonous consistency in the colors he had worn when she first saw him: always the gray pants, on rare occasions the dull blue coat changed for a gray one of the same corduroy material. He began to wear a long gray trenchcoat in the fall when it was still much too early for it, and he carried it to class with him religiously for the rest of the year, regardless of how beautiful the day might be. Sometimes she saw him wearing a blue beret in addition to the trenchcoat. One cold morning, when he entered the union building at coffee hour, this bit of attire brought him several hands of dubious applause, during which he could only smile awkwardly, almost sheepishly. The coat and the beret were both souvenirs of his service overseas in the second war, she heard it said. One rumor alluded to a British fiancee he had lost during this time in the bombing raids on London. At any rate, he had never married, and as might be expected for a man his age who lived with his mother, he walked amid whispers of perversity and disgrace.

Yet all that first year Elaine was never troubled by anything derogatory she heard about Dr. Shelley. She had no close friends, and she might have been lonely had it not been for Dr. Shelley, who kept her mind reeling with higher thought as she trudged from the dormitory to her classes and back. He had awakened in her an awareness that the earth she trod was covered with a gray film of sorrow, the earth on which sensitive people like Dr. Shelley in their gray trenchcoats suffered most. "*Lacrimae rerum*," Dr. Shelley had called it. "The tears of things." But it was a suffering which made them beautiful, and even in the bleakest winter she walked with a secret ecstacy at her heart. She was deeply grateful to him for having somehow made her life more meaningful than it had ever been before.

The following fall when Elaine returned she joined a sorority and did not live in the dormitory. This she did solely at the insistence of her mother, who was perturbed about her lack of social interests. Elaine, she pointed out, was after all an attractive girl. With her new social life forced upon her Elaine found her time for Dr. Shelley and higher thought regrettably diminished. She was not even able to schedule a class from him. She had instead a course in the English novel from a Dr. Cecil, an absentminded old professor near retirement who reminded Elaine of Mr. Dithers in the comic strips. Squinting behind his spectacles, he made frustrated little gestures as he tried to express himself about Dickens and George Eliot, sometimes forgetting where he was and unable to finish his sentences. His trousers were always badly in need of a pressing, and on some days Elaine could not decide whether he was wearing flesh-colored socks or had forgotten them altogether. For all his ineptness, he occasionally made spontaneous remarks which she noticed she did not forget.

She managed to visit Dr. Shelley now and then at his office, a thinly partitioned room in the basement of the old building where he had taught her freshman English. There she would descend a short stairway and cross the concrete floor of a hallway which always seemed to be cleanly mopped and to smell faintly of ammonia. At the end of the hallway she would knock lightly on the door which bore a blue index card with his typewritten name and title: "Homer Shelley, Assistant Professor of English."

She usually found him alone during his office hours. When she knocked she would hear him sing "Come in," and as she opened the door he would be turning in the swivel chair at his desk, saying, "Come in, Miss Summerfield," shyly and sincerely. Elaine would sit in a chair beside his desk. Light was admitted through a single window at ground level where the mournful leaves were piled all winter. It was a narrow little room, crowded with smoke and made narrower by the shelves of books on either side of it. His eyes were often red, and on his desk there was usually a full ashtray and a stack of themes to be graded. He always offered her a cigarette, and she always refused, referring once to an asthmatic condition.

Most of the reserve she had felt in his presence the year before was gone, and she talked with him quite frankly, usually about the books she read—*Walden*, *Of Human Bondage*, even Hazlitt's *Liber Amoris*, all of which he had recommended to her. He listened sympathetically, beaming with pride over the progress of his pupil. One afternoon she confided to him that after his own classes Dr. Cecil's course had proved a disappointment to her, but Dr. Shelley did not seem complimented. He only looked thoughtful and said sadly, "Not so long ago that old gentleman was one of my professors." He rose and faced the window, turning his back to her, and she heard him speak again, softly, "Life is a bitter jest." The light pouring through the rectangular window seemed to swallow him, and she wanted to see his face, for his phrase was so worn and theatrical that she was not at all certain, at that instant, of the depth of feeling she thought she knew in him.

Elaine did not call on Dr. Shelley again that year. She had achieved considerable popularity and circulated in the choicest party circles. Never, however, did she permit any indication of serious romantic attachment, if any existed. At the end of the spring term she overheard someone say that Dr. Shelley was going to spend his summer in Mexico with a promising young writer on campus, a boy whom Elaine had seen leaving his office at one of her visits. With an innuendo which brought smiles, Elaine inquired what was to become of his mother, and someone explained that Dr. Shelley's mother had died.

Elaine did not see Dr. Shelley at registration when she returned the following September at the start of her junior year. Another professor had to approve her program for her. She thought perhaps he had not come back from Mexico, but after the first month of the term she saw him one day in the hallway as he stepped out of a classroom. He seemed pale and weary. He saw her and obviously wished to speak to her, but he was caught in the crush of the between-class crowd and could not approach her as she moved away. After that she would see him now and then in the library searching for a book or driving his little blue car through the campus, always alone. She did not think about him much, and when she did she realized that just as she had lost the reserve his presence had inspired in her the first year, so now she had lost her respect for him. Even the admittedly brilliant lectures now seemed tainted. They were sonorous and rhetorical still, but they had lost the weight of content. She thought of him as her colleagues must have thought of him, and she understood now the scorn the graduate students had always had for him. She thought of him as a kind of machine that performed on the kinetic fuel of habit, used to provoke freshmen into thought year after year with the same stylized lectures, capable of draining the color from his cheeks when he wanted to show emotion.

Elaine knew that she owed her new evaluation of Dr. Shelley to her increased contact with the world, but she found herself equally disillusioned with that world. She still rode the party merry-go-round halfheartedly, but she had lost the sense of excitement of the year before. She had been the object of the attentions of two very different young men, the one an athlete, the other a soft-looking boy who studied the violin. But she was rude to the one and cold to the other, and eventually she discouraged them both.

The thought of close ties made her uneasy, for she sensed that they led to marriage, obscurity, and too much comfort, perhaps even the death of the soul that Dr. Shelley had once oratorically lamented. She missed the daily zest which he used to instill in her life, but she was aware that she was no longer a freshman and that turning to him would be fruitless. She would never have done so had she not run across a thin volume of poetry in the library stacks one evening near the end of the year.

The book seemed almost unused, and the author was Homer Shelley. The poems themselves were tense, often skeptical, full of losses and the sense of change, of darkness and light contending—*Theories of Light*, Dr. Shelley had titled the book. In one poem were two lines which caused a rush of insight:

I let the lit world be my beauty
While it lasts, though I am beast.

Elaine imagined Dr. Shelley wandering forlornly, unable to reveal his true being, awaiting some miracle to redeem him from his enigmatic and lonely world.

Searching further for his literary accomplishments, she found him among the contributors to an anthology of war stories which seemed the obscure brainchild of its pacifist editor, but Dr. Shelley's story—which was titled simply "Journeys" and which made little use of plot—was a disappointment to her after the poetry.

Still, Dr. Shelley had awakened her again to a world of hidden wonder and beauty, a world which only genuine feeling could have enabled him to perceive. She saw him again shimmering in the light that poured through his office window, and she saw a striving idealism or innocence in him which accounted for his occasional theatricality. She was ashamed of her own cynicism for supposing it to be shallowness. Sensing she had bitten the hand that had fed her she lingered on that summer to take the course he was offering in Romantic Poetry.

Dr. Shelley confided to his class at the outset that the subject was his favorite, yet somehow the course did not prove to be everything Elaine had looked forward to, for she was unable to connect Dr. Shelley with the poet she had discovered in the library stacks. He explained one day to his class the great and little-understood labor of the poet, and she surmised from his remarks and the tone of his voice that he was no longer able to write a poem.

Elaine knew that Dr. Shelley was working hard to revive her, as though he sensed her need and his own and saw a way to fulfill both. His eyes were clearer than she had ever seen them and his whole body seemed remarkably rested. She went to his office again, and he would call on her at the sorority house and they would walk in the rain-washed twilights. He lived near the university in an apartment with an outside staircase and a garret window, and he took her there after a walk one evening to listen to his collection of classical music. He turned the lights down low and in the dark poured the magic notes into her soul like the rain on the famished earth. At such moments he would look as though he wanted to confide to her something desperate, but he never made untoward advances, nor did she expect him to. Coming out of class one day he put his hand on the back of her neck, but the venture surprised her and she could see that he at once felt awkward about it. He could only smile sheepishly and mumble something irrelevant.

Sometimes they stopped in the union for coffee after a walk, but one Friday evening he took her to a cafeteria which he preferred near the edge of the campus. It was subterranean, off a plaza in a shopping center, at the bottom of one of Southwest City's tallest buildings—the Prudential Building crowned by a neon Rock of Gibraltar. They stopped at a little pond in the plaza to watch the dark forms of carp darting among the water lights. Music from a hidden speaker drifted between the buildings—Elaine recognized it as the theme from *A Summer Place*—and at the far end of the plaza a man was trying to interest some straggling shoppers in a shiny new sportscar on display. They descended then to the cafeteria, a clean, carpeted place, but nearly deserted and ultimately pitiful, and something made Elaine recall the Rock of Gibraltar outlined against the blackness of the night.

When they left, he stopped her suddenly in front of the big glass doorway, and pointing to their reflections he whispered, "Look, Elaine, you're beautiful, you're beautiful." She tried to think of something nice to say, but when she looked at his reflection she just said "Thank you" very quietly and continued out the door. He stood for a moment in the doorway, and as the door swung back and hit him in the stomach he let out an absurd little grunt.

In class the following day, as he was explicating Keats' "Ode to a Nightingale," his voice seemed slightly hoarse as he drew near the end. He looked directly at Elaine then as he had done once before, his face whitened again, and he murmured with subdued passion, "Fled is that music:—Do I wake or sleep?" It seemed to Elaine that he wept almost imperceptibly, but he carried on without faltering, stoically. She tried to find the exhilaration she had known before, but it was something darker and heavier that passed over her heart. She saw him as the strange machine she had envisioned earlier, or the absurd buffoon she had seen in the door of the cafeteria. He couldn't restore any of the beautiful insight to her life, and she went home feeling more hollow than ever at the end of the term.

In September Elaine returned disenchanted for her final year at the university. She left the sorority to move back into the dormitory and proceeded to withdraw from all of her acquaintances of the previous years. She sought to avoid Dr. Shelley altogether, but one bright October day on the old campus she saw him under the yellowing cottonwoods where the crows that arrived in the fall were beginning to gather. An ineffectual scarecrow in his gray trenchcoat, he stood listening respectfully to an elderly man who gestured with his hands as he talked—Elaine could see that it was Dr. Cecil, her old teacher. They parted as she watched, and Dr. Shelley walked away sadly, looking at the ground.

Then one day after class she was walking down a crowded hallway when she felt a hand on the back of her neck. She realized at once that it was Dr. Shelley: he was a man of habit and could not learn from experience. She turned on him with a "Get your hands off me!" look and he could only smile sheepishly and mumble something irrelevant. He was too painfully aware of himself to be really innocent, she decided. He left her alone after that.

Although nothing seemed to interest her, Elaine was not entirely alone that first part of her senior year. She was courted rather steadily by a young engineering student who was to take a graduate degree at midyear. He had struck up a conversation

with her at the library for their initial acquaintance, and she per-
mitted his attentions out of curiosity. He combed his black hair
neatly, yet there was something vaguely absentminded about his
appearance: he was a door that should be open or closed left
standing carelessly ajar.

He took her to movies, and one night they sat in the union
and watched a western on television. Elaine marveled that a
graduate student could become absorbed in such a thing. Trying
to sleep that night, uneasy about all the lost hours she had spent
with him, she was still tormented by the ebb and flow of horses'
hooves, now rising to loud pounding, now ebbing away to faint
thumping. It was Dr. Shelley, she reasoned, who had led her
into this limbo. He had urged her to question her existence, and
now she dangled on the suspicion that it was inconsequential.
She suspected, moreover, that he had known as much all along.
She fell asleep at last, but she found herself sitting up in bed in
the dark beyond midnight, shaken by a dream, an experience
that was at once an illumination and a part of reality.

In the dream, she made her way through thinly partitioned
hallways with concrete floors, in complex pattern, like a maze,
dimly lighted. She saw the ghosts of two girls in nightgowns flit-
ter around a distant corner. There was even a faint smell of ammonia, but then she detected that something was burning, an
odor which grew more perceptible, though never strong. She
paused at the head of a corridor which seemed to lead nowhere,
and she heard, barely audible, a slow popping of flame from behind its farthest door. She was not consciously seeking, yet she
knew what awaited her, and when she opened the door softly,
there was the man. There was what was left of the man, beyond
help. He lay in the corner with what might have been left of his
face turned to the wall, his hair gone, his ashy body still burning
slowly in the faint popping of the slender flame, and as she stood
in the doorway the eyes came slowly round and found her eyes.
Then for a full minute she saw only the eyes, dark, lambent,
smoldering with fear and compassion, pleading with her to look,

pitying her for seeing. She looked, and she heard her own heart pleading, "Don't be afraid," and then, "I know, I know." Then the flame began to pop, and when she looked into the charred remains there was no soul, no spirit, but only the ruined framework, the smoldering fuselage of a man. Then she was awake, still peering, her heart asking who? Was it herself, the whole hallucination a product of her own nervous system, or had she seen the death of Dr. Shelley, his life consumed before his very eyes while he toiled with his freshman themes in his obscure little office? She understood something of the pain of consciousness which Dr. Shelley lived with, and she knew that all his sermons about the "heart that can aspire" and even the beautiful images of light in his poetry were not enough in the face of his despair.

When Thanksgiving recess arrived her engineer reminded her that he was to graduate in January and confessed that his intentions with her had become quite serious: he did not want to leave without her. He invited her to come home with him to meet his parents, and he explained that he had been offered a job upon graduation with a big oil company. Elaine pictured him with oil stains forever under his fingernails and in his already greasy hair. Feeling herself pushed, she told him she did not love him and never could. To her relief, he left her alone from then on. She saw him only once again, briefly, as she passed him on a teeming sidewalk on her way to class. He gave her a little wounded glance which she thought was calculated to let her know that he was nourishing a broken heart.

Elaine remained withdrawn after that. Universities seemed cumbersome affairs, vast mating grounds, populated for the most part by people who considered themselves superior to porpoises, and who wanted to step unscathed into jobs with big oil companies and send their offspring back in turn. It was almost Christmas recess by then, and when she made train reservations to go

home she decided to make them one way. She would act spon-
taneously. She would simply leave, not bothering to withdraw
through official channels. Nothing, she thought, would give her
greater satisfaction.

On the eve of her departure she thought of a farewell to Dr.
Shelley, knowing she would probably never see him again. She
might have dismissed the thought, however, had he not anticipated her. At noon the dorm supervisor handed her a note he
had sent, requesting her to call at his office. The dormitory was
fast being evacuated for the holidays, and she went first to her
room to pack. Then she went.

She crossed the old campus where some of the crows that
had come with the fall still lingered in the bare elms and cottonwoods. They cawed at her with excitement and wheeled under
the white winter sky. She crossed the kissing bridge over the
little pond and stared for a moment at the motionless green
water. She descended the familiar short stairway and crossed the
cleanly mopped hallway that smelled faintly of ammonia. She
knocked lightly at his door.

"Come in," she heard him sing. He was alone. "Please sit
down." He smiled shyly behind red-rimmed eyes and motioned
to the chair beside his desk. He wore gray gabardine pants and a
faded blue corduroy coat.

Elaine sat down. Dr. Shelley stood up, momentarily silent,
and looked out the ground-level window where the yellowed
leaves were piled.

"Well," he said finally, "I thought I'd better see how you
were doing. I *am* your advisor, you know."

"I know," Elaine said. There was, she knew, small comfort
in her voice.

"I wish you'd come more often. This is your last year, you
know, and then what will you do?"

"I don't know," Elaine said. "It's hard to say."

He seemed puzzled. "You need this holiday," he offered.
"When you come back—"

"I'm not coming back." She decided it was necessary, and she saw her chance.

"If it's something financial," he began helplessly, "I could help you get a scholarship, or something."

"It's not financial," Elaine said.

Silence.

"Well, I feared as much," he began again. "I just wish you had come to see me more often. I get lonely here, you know." He tried to be light, but his smile was tense. He began to fidget with a paperweight on his desk.

"I've been awfully busy," Elaine said. His intentions were painfully obvious to her now. She wished she had never come, and the room seemed more narrow than she had remembered it. He held out a pack of cigarettes and she accepted one, grateful for the diversion. She inhaled from the trembling flame of his lighter. She handled it awkwardly, without experience.

Dr. Shelley pursued, forcing himself on, as if he had no choice. "What I mean is, I really do get lonely."

Elaine tried to concentrate on the titles of the books in the shelf beside her. Dr. Shelley was concentrating on his paperweight as he spoke. He wasn't smiling anymore.

"You've changed so much, Elaine. You're not the girl I used to know. . . . I come to you still hoping that I can find her. I don't know where else to go."

More silence. He took up the echo of his own words, "I don't know where else to go." He began to seem beside himself in the little hoarse voice of his passion. "I'm lonely, Elaine. You see I'm completely alone now."

Elaine felt her breathing tighten. She snuffed out her cigarette in his ashtray.

"I have to go," she said.

Dr. Shelley's cheeks drained white. He set the paperweight down and looked at her in the face for the first time. He spoke quietly.

"Don't you like me, Elaine?" Then, feeling herself recoil, she heard him add, "Don't you like men?"

The words soared high above her, then found their mark, deftly like a mortar. She bolted up and looked at him swiftly, dumbly. She sought the door, blind in her rage, her chest constricted. At the door of the building she stamped her foot down suddenly and turned back toward his office. She wanted to look at him and shout "You beast, you beast, you freak!" but when she reached his door she caught her breath. He was slumped on his desk, delicately turning her cigarette in his fingers, contemplating the lipstick stains on it. Her words would not come, and she turned again and began to walk rapidly away, weeping almost imperceptibly.

At the railroad station the next morning, Elaine boarded her train and sat by the window. The sun was about to clear the mountains. It would be a blue sky.

Then she discovered, in the little crowd that stood before the terminal in the last phase of dawn, a familiar face turned toward her, the whitened face of Dr. Shelley. As the train began to move she had the feeling all at once that she had been wrong about him, that she had been terribly unkind. He did not raise his hand, nor did she. He just stood looking at her, and then he was gone. The train passed under an overpass, and Elaine had a glimpse of her own pale face.

The Walking Stick

If I walk into the wood
As far as I can walk, I come to my own door,
The door of the House in the Wood.
—Randell Jarrell, The Lost World

WALK LONG ENOUGH AND FAR ENOUGH AND WE WERE SURE to come to something in the end. To what, I'm sure we knew not. Perhaps it was ourselves we sought, the house in the wood forsaken long ago, never quite forgotten. San Anselmo, the little town where I grew up, was a town for walkers, or so I came to think, I suppose because I was one myself, perhaps the most inveterate. There was also Howard Rosensweig, who left the figure of his solitary personage, bent against our twilight skies, indelibly etched on my young mind. There was my father, too. Saturnine by nature, he nevertheless seemed driven by an inner nerve, a kind of suppressed but never quite spent anxiety, so that he lacked Howard's forlorn resignation.

And now in this glow of summer's end, here in this solemn city perhaps a hundred miles and half my life removed from San Anselmo, there's still another walker in my streets, a long, lank, slope-shouldered, haunting kind of man, a man I've named the Walking Stick. Like him, I've come to know that there are those of us who stray, lost from the moving, visible world that most men live in, or rather those for whom, in one sense or another, the world is lost. Such men are we.

As for me, I formed the habit young. Sunlight on walls, on fences, trees, the luminous clouds at evening no one seemed to notice—in my young manhood, these were enough to lure me to the streets and drive me on. Much younger, and even in a time when I walked little on my own, my father took me with him on the mesa out beyond our house. Together there, I in the wheelbarrow he pushed so tirelessly, we found and traced each semblance of a path in that wide, light-stricken land I later found it hard to live without.

When I was older, we turned westward to the mountains, and packing fishing gear or sometimes water colors, hiked the river to a high and heady place where it divided, boulder-strewn and lined with willow brush.

"Trout like the shade," my father would explain, and take the fork he called Dark Canyon, a quiet, green-shadowed corridor with dripping granite walls. The other fork was toward the sun, a trail we hardly ever took unless we came to paint. I never saw the end of either trail but much preferred the one we seldom took, the path that seemed to open into light, toward places one returns from with the sound of mountain water still falling through his mind.

"Besides," my father added once, forsaking sunlight for the shade, "this way is real. The other way's a lie."

When I was older still, and old enough, perhaps, to want to know too much, my father turned away and walked in solitude.

In solitude, the Walking Stick is walking on the edge of my existence. I've seen him in the corner of my eye. I've named him, yes, but for myself alone. I'll never know his own. To see him is to know, somehow, such knowledge is forbidden; to speak with him, an act past contemplation.

There's a splash of color at the top of him, a yellow baseball cap that hides his face in shadow. In autumn now, he's donned a denim jacket to combat the wind. His workman's pants are denim too, loose fitting on long legs, which, if like the rest of him, are hard and thin. He favors one of them—as I recall, the right one—and reminds me vaguely of a man on stilts, though wherever he is going, he makes long-practiced, steady progress.

I see him day and night, whenever least expected, though we're both drawn out, I've come to believe, by the same kinds of weather. This dripping evening in November, with a high fog blotting the night sky, I've logged miles on the silent pavements, and then, near home, on the street I am crossing, I hear foot-steps retreating half a block away. It's he, I know at once, and turning to look, I see I am not wrong. I pause to watch until the night mist swallows his disappearing heels.

Or when the rain has turned to sleet, or when the wind has bared the moon and chilled stars in the clear winter sky, there he is, ambling along in the streets of my mind when I least expect to see him. Yet he is real, too, carrying as often as not a brown sack of real groceries to that nearby half block of run-down but real apartments where I surmise he lives—I've never seen him entering or leaving a domicile of any kind, but I surmise again it's small and sparsely fitted out, wherever it may be. And I sur-mise he earns a meagre living for himself, employed someplace like the nearby city shops—I've seen him headed there, lunch pail in hand, on more than one occasion. The evening walks toward Texas Street suggest he's wont to eat in seedy restaurants there, though I'm troubled to imagine him in one, and so engag-ing in the necessary words to speak a preference for dinner, for, as for preferences, he has none.

Yet he is real, if from the real world lost.

A lost man, my father turned from me and walked in soli-tude, or so it seemed to me, and to my mother, too. A book of

73

road maps was his consolation. I believe you could have set the house on fire and with a road map charmed him to a studied immobility. It was to him what pipe and tobacco are to another. But worse, I suppose. Like alcohol to those who find it hard to do without.

He was a man of contradictions. He loved the land we'd come to, but if he talked with us at all, it would be to urge us further west, to California, perhaps, or failing to convince us, he'd speak of going "home" again to West Virginia—the very place, my mother would remind him, where he and I had almost suffocated in the throes of asthma. His restlessness, that never quite buried anxiety, betrayed her own exasperation. They quarrelled, and then long silences ensued. It was as if, exiled from what he called his home, my father exiled himself again to solitude. When he went up to Dark Canyon, he went alone.

He set his painting aside—gave it up, to tell the truth. From the garage studio he gradually fashioned the shop where he strung tennis rackets, and there he spent much of his time. If he had any friends, they were those few tennis playing acquaintances, like Howard Rosensweig, who occasionally visited him there in the evenings, and if he talked much with anyone, it was with them. My own room, converted with the aid of a set of bunk beds, a desk and chair from the compact storage room at the back end of the house, had a common wall with the garage, and there, lying awake at night in my upper bunk, I'd hear the wayward bits of their sometimes serious talk, such as the bit that comes to mind even now.

"What do *you* think, John?" a musing, pensive voice inquired.

Perhaps a half a minute passed, and then the answer followed, quiet but clear.

"I think that when we die," my father said, "we go to the grave and we rot."

From such stray ends of overheard conversation I formed a

piecemeal portrait, but it was another portrait, a portrait in bronze-colored ink hanging from the wall of my room in a bronze frame, which taught me, at least in retrospect, a less tenuous knowledge of my father. It was the delicate, clean and sensitive face of a turbaned man, half East Indian, I suppose, but godlike, too, for in the clean simplicity of its lines it was not unlike the picture of the bust of Apollo I had seen in my history book. Inquiry revealed from my mother that it was something my father had done as a student in college. I must have contemplated it often, no doubt more often than I was aware, though I could not, if asked, account for its fate. My father's face, by my time, was somewhat thin and haggard—his bout with asthma had been sudden and serious, and there had been, I'm sure, the disappointments of the artist and the teacher, the extent of which I would only later appreciate. And it was in retrospect, too, that I came to see a resemblance between that face and the one in the bronze frame which hung from the wall of my room. It was a beautiful face—in its way, an inspiring face. It made me think not of dark canyons, but of sunlight on falling mountain water. It had nobility. And the resemblance was there. It was neither obvious nor intended, I'm sure, but it was there.

Yes, my father must have been a man beset by contradictions, the confirmation of my soul.

The confirmation of my soul, the Walking Stick has disappeared. Deep into winter now, for days, weeks, a month or more, I've missed him. Our paths may not have crossed. More likely, I suspect, something has happened. I imagine him ill, alone, confined by himself to bed, with resignation waiting out a long, persistent fever that burns in his already dessicated body. Or perhaps, discovered at last by a concerned landlady, he lies by now in the bed of a hospital, of the one that lights the hill at night on Santa Fe Street. There between white sheets his lank frame lies supine, his unseen eyes scanning the sterile walls and the white ceiling. He has no visitors, of course, and if any try to call, they don't know whom to ask for.

A month or more ago, I lifted my eyes, and there he stood. Down the long blind wall of the variety store he'd ambled in that steady but stilt-like walk to the corner across the street, and there he stood in the gray afternoon, side-stepping my glance until he was half hidden behind the traffic signal post, his jacket open, his eyes, sheltered beneath the bill of his yellow cap, cast down the street. When the light changed, we crossed the street and passed. I meant no harm, to be sure, and least of all any discourtesy, but as we passed I sought his face, for how could I do otherwise? His eyes, averted down and away, were not the eyes of one who hides, nor one who seeks, but those of one who used to seek. Alluding to the world of flesh and suffering and bone, they yet elude my last inquiry.

Was it, or was it not a sidelong glance he shot me as we passed? I looked at him too long, no doubt; since then, expected him too much. Deep into winter now, I miss him sorely. Home from my solitary walks, I sit down at my solitary table, and see the trembling of my solitary hands. I miss him as I miss the sun.

Missing them sorely, I went home to spend a few days of leave with my parents early in the war. I'd outgrown all traces of my asthma by then, but my father's lingered and, when he was called up later for possible induction, earned him rejection.

They were alone, if living together, and my father spent most of his time in his garage, converted by then to a full-scale tennis shop, having abandoned his teaching. I'd never known him to drink before, but at dinner time he'd come into the house with a tumbler of bourbon in hand and asked me if I cared to join him.

The morning of the day I left, he went out after breakfast and began to load his car with fishing gear. My mother, seeing me wonder, came back from the kitchen and sat with me at the table where I lingered. She looked at me, hesitated, then forced herself to speak.

"You know, Sonny, we're leaving San Anselmo." She stressed the "know," just slightly, as though the explanation she conveyed were something I should have taken for granted. Perhaps I should have, but I hadn't.

"He wants to go back to West Virginia, he says. You know I don't. He wants to be alone, I believe."

"It does seem like that sometimes," I offered.

She searched my face in that consoling way she had, and sadly—for my sake, I saw—she added, "We're going to leave, Sonny, but not together."

Speechless, I stood and wandered toward the door. I heard a car door close, walked out and tried to watch my father arranging his gear in the trunk.

"Dark Canyon?" I inquired.

"Dark Canyon," he confirmed. He straightened slowly, and, face averted, added, "Want to come?"

It was an invitation I'd not anticipated. I looked eastward where the morning light was flooding the vast mesa beyond our house. I knew no words could circumvent the knot in my throat, but I wanted to ask if we couldn't choose instead the mesa where the light was shining, retrace just one of those wheelbarrow trails we'd made there years ago.

"I guess not," I managed at last, and I gestured helplessly toward the house where my mother was, toward the mesa beyond.

He extended his hand, and for the first time that I could remember he fixed me with a sad, deliberate look, a look that said, "Live long enough and you'll begin to understand." His face seemed strangely open, discolored slightly about the cheeks and eyes.

We shook hands. He got in the car without looking back, started the engine and eased away on the gravel drive. I turned east again, wondering couldn't we wait till the war was over when the three of us could stroll there together, dissolve our differences, however grievous, in that warm, generous, land-glancing light of the seemingly endless prairie.

But my father was gone, and I knew I'd lost that man forever.

Lost almost forever, the man I named the Walking Stick is gone, I fear, with winter. The day, a Sunday in the earliest spring, is tentatively fair. A cold wind blows, white clouds are scudding, but the sun casts longed-for accents on a land of light and shadow. Toward morning's end, with church bells tolling, I labor up Santa Fe Street after a long and aimless wandering. Against the old stone wall that borders the hospital grounds, where the shadows of skeletal locust trees dance in dazzling light, there's a flash of yellow. I lift my eyes, and there he is. My heart leaps, yet saddens, too, to see him now: he *has* been ill, I know. His gait is slower, more laborious, his right leg favored more than ever. He picks his way carefully now, this man who loves to walk, who cannot help walking. The invisible stilts he walks on seem about to break beneath him. Like a spring colt, he seems to test his limbs, yet there is nothing coltish about him. He is a grateful but cautious convalescent, glad to be walking again in the world of spring light, glad enough to be alive.

He is there but a moment or two before he passes into an alley, some byway of life I won't pursue. He is there but a moment or two, a patchwork of light and shadow himself, an anonymous man caught momentarily in an amorphous figment of shadow and dazzling light on an old stone wall. But before he passes he pauses and turns toward me, and I can see by the tilt on the bill of his yellow cap that he gazes, momentarily, directly at me, and unless I'm mistaken, there's the slightest of thin-lipped smiles on his face. He is there but a moment or two, and then he is gone.

Sensing the end of something, I search my heart to find

what's left of him—more likely, what remains of me. Live long enough, and one begins to understand. I see the silent, self-effacing man and understand humility. There's goodness there as well, an unassuming goodness that the world has never marked, and never will. Beyond that, something more, something setting him apart: a certain dessicated, self-denied, consumed divinity, a kind of immortality, perhaps? No, I'm wrong to think it. The sadness of his smile suggested otherwise, his very passing pointing toward mortality. I've watched him pass, and watched the passing of the last companion of my life.

Journeys

An Interlude by
Dr. Shelley

I

WHEN THE FOG LIFTED THE SHIP LIMPED IDLY INTO THE HAR-
bor. They managed to dock and disembark. Bent under
his gear, he fell in with his comrades when the sergeant gave
them a halfhearted command to muster. The sergeant said the
colonel would want to address them, but the colonel responded
with a singularly hapless wave of his hand, not unlike the tail of
a grazing horse waving at a fly.

The city remained, factories, buildings, heroic statuary, but
at the pier there were not even the handful of faithful wives that
he had imagined would be there, excluding, of course, his own,
although her name was on his lips.

It was October. The war was over, even though no one
seemed to care. They were given three days of liberty.

2

In the city he learned that in the beginning people had
scattered in all directions, seeking their separate sanctuaries, so

that one marveled, if he were among those who had lingered, at the sudden peace, the near silence.

Freeways were now all but deserted, and at the bottom of steel canyons traffic lights continued to function, senselessly, futilely; yet it was days before he adjusted to crossing against the "DON'T WALK" signal, to crossing anywhere at will. Except for electronically timed whistles and sirens, the city had subsided to silence. Ironically, the air was cleansing itself.

At the airport he noticed that the miles of runway lights still flickered on at dusk, and over the terminal he saw the flags of several nations curled idly in the amorphous breeze.

3

On the fourth day, after mustering in again, he was told that he would shortly have to stand trial. Then they knew, he told himself, but to remove any doubt he asked why, and they told him it was for not killing a man.

He had been given the unwanted assignment of moving a prisoner who was to be interrogated. Late in the day they had rested while a convoy of trucks and men crossed their path. The afternoon sun caught the steel of helmets and weapons, and some of the men yelled obscenities at the prisoner. Dust swirled and engines droned and cursed, and the convoy crawled away toward the horizon. When it was almost out of sight, he told the prisoner to "take off." The man hesitated. He told him again, and watched the man look uncertainly toward the woods. In the fading light he motioned with his weaponless hand toward the woods and turned his back on his prisoner to look after the convoy again. Where it had been there was now only a little cloud of dust that hung above the road in front of the sun. Her name had risen in his mind. He never conjured her image, but her name was often in his mind like an image.

When he had turned around again, the man was gone.

4

In the city one morning he was attracted by the ringing voice of a street-corner orator. He approached and discovered that he was the man's only audience. The orator, a bearded man with a lantern at his side, eyed him suspiciously. Deciding to continue, he told the story of a friend, a teacher who had become disenchanted and quit his calling to take a job cleaning out motel rooms. "It was what people really wanted," the orator disclosed, "and he was the happier for his decision, feeling at last that he was doing something useful."

Here the bearded man, disdaining to say more, gave him a quick neurotic glance, hoisted his lantern, and stalked away down an empty street.

5

Later in the week he awaited his turn before the magistrate. The people who were appearing before him—and among them he recognized the bearded orator with his lantern—did not seem to be on trial, but instead were complaining to the presiding magistrate about the most trivial things: the poor quality of this kind of coffee and that kind of tobacco, the shortage of bananas and live lobsters. No one in the sparse courtroom was taking them seriously, and indeed the magistrate himself seemed to be nodding with boredom or extreme fatigue.

When the lantern-bearer's turn came he announced that he had come to protest "the general cruelty toward animals observable throughout the city." He related how animals still locked up in the zoo were starving, and he told the story of the silver fox who, with desperate paws, had worn away the paint on the gate of his cage. There was a ripple of amusement, but the laughter was nervous, as if on edge.

"Is that all?" asked the magistrate, somewhat bewildered after the speaker had paused.

"No." The speaker waited again until the air had cleared. "Spring comes, and the earth does not turn green again." His attitude had turned wistful. "I can remember mornings when the birds were singing."

People stared, and then someone laughed openly.

"Birds were singing," someone mocked as he turned to a comrade. They were military men—officers, as one could see by the braid on their epaulets.

Here the magistrate seemed to rouse himself, and strutting his manliness, he pointed out that although the plaintiff would have to do without his "customary birdsong," he would nonetheless be obliged to "speak to the point—at least in this courtroom." A trace of emotion had come to his voice.

The bearded speaker, who had been uttering dream-like phrases such as "being in high mountains," "a flight of birds against the sky," "a tree in the changing weather," now seemed to bite his lip.

"In short," the magistrate was finishing sternly, "your argument seems the most confused and sentimental this court has yet encountered." He stood up then, perhaps preparing to dismiss the hearing, but the lantern-bearer was not yet finished. Setting the lantern to his well oiled shirt, he contrived a burst of flame that won back his reluctant audience, suddenly awed by the heroic serenity with which he employed his device.

Pounding a gavel, the magistrate ordered him doused with the proper chemicals, but by the time these were found it was apparent to everyone that the man was beyond recall. The magistrate himself was in a state of collapse, and had to be assisted from his courtroom.

6

His own trial, of course, was postponed. Hearing that the magistrate had never recovered, he was told he would have to await orders from his commanding officer, but by the time of their third muster this gentleman was himself conspicuously absent, and among his dwindling company there was a rumor that he was likely to remain so.

He thought often about the death of the lantern-bearer. Whether he had died in pain or not he could not say. He had given no indication of pain, but he could not imagine such a death being less than unbearable. He thought about the parable of the teacher he had heard the man reciting to himself. What did it mean? Not everyone could make such adjustments in life, he considered, and as long as official bureaus had remained intact to report, there had been an alarming increase of suicides.

He began to think of home, and one morning he awoke with words in his mouth:

Among those mountains
Where the water-liar sleeps
He made a bargain
With a man he did not keep.

He recognized the poet's symptom, and though the words made him uneasy he was nevertheless grateful for them.

7

His uneasiness mounted, and he punctuated all his observations with questions about himself. He began to form sympathies with the leftover faces he found on the "WANTED" notices in the abandoned post offices. He spoke only when spoken to, which was seldom indeed.

He sat one day within the white walls of an art museum, wondering at what was happening. In place of the sense of moderation he found exaggeration and mere size. One of the chambers of the museum was dominated by a sculpture of a man and woman in the act of copulating. The woman's hips, especially, seemed exaggerated, but what impressed him most profoundly were their heads, arched upward on serpentine necks, expressionless, faceless, mere bullet-shaped abstractions. Yet in those bullet-shaped heads, he thought, the sculptor had captured the seeds of something illuminating.

8

He was up one morning at dawn for a walk through the city. It was November then. A lonely man who spit something bloody into the gutter approached him as if to beg some change, then changed his mind with a scornful shrug.

Further along he came upon a man who was threatening a dog, cursing him for no apparent reason. The dog trotted off as if nothing had happened, or as if he'd expected it to happen, walking the way dogs walk, slightly sidewise, his hindquarters wagging out of line. He could see, he thought, the dog's resentment, his dislike for man in general.

And there in that cold and bloomless morning he felt he had made a discovery. It was, no doubt, too late for survival even in the sparse places of the planet, but if anyone cared there was nowhere any evidence of the fact.

9

He climbed up the stairs of an office building, seeking an elderly lady he had once corresponded with in the city. She had been a literary agent to him, though she had never placed any of his work. The building seemed deserted, and he did not really expect to find her.

Yet surprisingly enough he found her in. She sat at her desk with her lunch spread before her, explaining that she practically lived in her office now—she didn't like to go out and her work was all that kept her going. He was surprised enough to ask "What work?" But seeing her reaction, a mixture of embarrassment and dread, he did not press the question. He offered her his new poem. She offered him lunch, but he declined.

He had to leave in a hurry. They shook hands. She watched from the window and saw him cross the street below. He entered a bookstore where men used to browse day and night in lewd magazines.

Still, she thought, there was such beauty in the young man. In the leanness of his face. He had said he did not usually eat lunch anyway. In the very way he held his hands.

She looked at the poem:

Remember this one as the one
Who lost his way:
Among those mountains
Where the water-liar sleeps
He made a bargain
With a man he did not keep,
Since when he falling
Feared the fall
He never saw, except as spirit
Is the child of consequence,
Condemned to life,
Not death, life
In this literal light.

10

He helped himself to a car that had been abandoned in the street. There were many such cars to be had, some where the dead driver lay slumped in the seat. He took to a once crowded freeway, and when it forked he kept to his right, heading west.

Days passed. The already blighted population was now

even more strikingly desecrated, but here and there someone eyed him cautiously as he drove through towns and villages across the leveling landscape. Occasionally a thin trail of smoke rose from a chimney into the winter sky.

He kept to the backroads, and at night he pulled off the roadside in out-of-the-way places to sleep in the car. At abandoned gas pumps he stopped to refuel when necessary. He had made no decision in the city, none that he was aware of, but now he was making his way west on this maze of backroads, the forgotten capillaries of a continent.

He drove through wheat fields that had gone to stubble. The land began to roll. The wheat gave way to dead grasslands, and there were close gray horizons under a cloud-darkened sky.

Then he knew he was going home, and somewhere within him there rose the half-formed hope that he would live until spring.

II

He headed south by west. There were little mountains, volcanic hills and buttes, rising at random above the plain. The older ones, worn by the weight of millions of years, sloped away gradually and evenly to the horizon in pleasing symmetry. They were small mountains and large mesa tops made from the waste of larger mountains which loomed in the distance further west.

He stopped when he came to a house he remembered, an old frame house with a fallen roof and glass broken and scattered about its floor. The paint on the low picket fence and the walls had peeled in the fierce sunlight. It sat brooding on that eastward rolling sea of gray-green hills under the vast light-stricken blue of the sky. Momentarily, he brooded with it.

And suddenly life flew out of the ruined windows, darting about his head and shoulders like rain in the wind, but under that unvarying blueness. Swallows—there must have been a thousand of them—defended their property daringly, but with unmistakable joy, it seemed to him. They made swift sallies about his head and, circling round again, careened on the silent pond beneath the ghost of a windmill behind the house.

He watched entranced, and then he left, feeling himself the trespasser now.

12

Except the swallows, he had not seen a living soul in more than a week. He had come upon red clay ravines with thin groves of tamarisk, where sometimes there remained a trace of water. Occasionally, near the waterbed, there grew a cotton-wood, but these seemed all to be dying. He remembered how their leaves would turn gold and glide down late in the year, some spinning heavily, others slowly and silently, hovering as if they were not going to fall at all. When he saw them he would catch his breath.

Crossing a ravine, he stopped the car and got out to explore it. Its bed curved away out of sight, and by following it he could see that the land, although seemingly level, was dropping. His feet twisted awkwardly on the red stones in the dry arroyo, but he followed for an hour and came upon one of those abrupt sur-prises of the high mesa country: there was a decline, not of great height, but enough so that he saw suddenly for a good distance across the mesa where the ravines looked like thin scars under the glancing light. A hundred yards ahead of him there was a knoll which offered a vantage point, and as he approached he saw, at the base of a weatherbeaten juniper further down the slope, something move. He looked carefully, pausing to catch his breath. It was a man, he thought, and he felt that he too had been seen. It seemed to him then that something was wrong.

Going down to him, he found a young Indian who had rested himself beneath the tree, and though he had moved but a minute ago, he was now quite dead.

13

The mesa turned yellow and arid, and he came upon the small, familiar city which he had barely the heart to look upon. From his hill, he stood looking over it, then focused his attention on a house with walls of white stucco that caught the light of the sun.

He was walking down a street that led to the house, when he thought he had seen something, something like a shadow, pause at the entrance and enter. He walked faster. He entered and began to search.

He knew the house intimately. As he went from room to room he imagined a thief. He came to the last room in the house, and there remained only one door to open. He opened it slowly, holding his breath . . . but there was no one.

He had seen something like a shadow—perhaps his own, it occurred to him. Through the familiar rooms and around the familiar corners of the house he grew up in he had stalked the most insidious of all thieves, a thief who would steal from him everything before he was through, everything.

14

He headed toward the mountains. The mountains were ominous, yet there had been a time when they were innocent and warm in his heart.

As a boy he had gone fishing in the mountains with his father. Near the river where it tumbled in a series of little falls, they had slept in the bed of a pickup truck with the roar of the rushing water in their heads. After one night he had wished that sound could always be there.

It was to such a place he had brought his wife-to-be not long after he had met her. She had often reminded him of it, recalling fondly some of the things he had said to her. He remembered them sitting together on a boulder above the stream, the sunlight on their faces and the noise of the water mingling with his own soft-spoken words.

In the mountain canyon darkness had come early. All day he had watched the wedge of blue sky at the end of the canyon with wisps of cloud drifting through it. Once, from the trail above, he looked down at her dangling her feet in a clear pool in the stream, and she turned around and looked up, and smiled at him. Through the haze of the sky, resounding from the rock-piled wall of the canyon, they heard the cry of a night hawk.

15

In the remains of an adobe village, at the foot of a mountain where mountains and mesa land met, he elected to stay until spring. He loved the sky here, and the clouds that gathered in the afternoons, and the winter light. He loved especially the mornings, the way the light rose in the scattered sky, the mesa loud with light. But behind him, above him, the snow and ice upon the mountain passes waited ominously. For as long as he was able he turned his back on these, and walked on the mesa.

He had seen nothing living until on one of his walks he flushed a dove. Watching the white band in its feathers flicker again and again with short bursts of frenetic energy, he could see it was sick or injured. He followed it as far as he was able, but it had soon concealed itself in the brush again.

He whistled a simple refrain, recognizing it as a signal, a kind of greeting which he had exchanged with a boyhood friend long ago. He did not know what brought it to his lips again, but he paused to listen, half expecting his answer from somewhere on the wide, light-flooded and lonely mesa.

16

Near the village he found one day a half-ruined road that led northeasterly to nowhere, unless to the dregs of a river, sunk deep in arroyos of gray clay and choked with tamarisk. Yet it persisted, he thought, and he faced the mountains then. He decided to explore the source of the river.

He attributed its source to a high, snowbound peak that reared its head above the range of mountains behind his house. At any rate, it seemed to be descending from that vicinity, for it entered the foothill and mesa country from a long and rock-bound canyon which twisted its way into the heart of the granite mountains.

He climbed into them as far as he could, but once in the mountains he found what seemed another river, whose clear waters shouted to him, siren-like, as they descended over rocks and boulders. Standing there alone in a singing and sun-lit pass, he remembered the water-liar, and looking upstream as far as he could, and beyond, where mountain backed mountain in a wilderness forbidding and interminable, he felt the hand of him upon his heart.

17

Again he awoke with words in his mouth:

We wake to the rain
And we hear the pounding of his heart.

They seemed like the purest poetry to him, like Indian words, and he hoped he would not lose the feeling they gave him. It had rained during the night, and the earth was fresh. It was spring.

He took to the highway again and climbed up the back-bone of the continent. The trees thinned to small drab pines that clung to the leaden walls and piles of granite. Reaching the crest, he began to drop too rapidly down the tortured highway and had to pump his brakes too frequently. Finally the descent altered and became less abrupt.

The highway picked up the course of a stream and meandered now between rounded hills, the shoulders of the mountains, covered with short grass and patches of scrub oak but otherwise bare. Now and then it crossed through meadows where the narrow river concealed itself behind borders of red willow. Near evening, at the end of one long meadow, at the juncture of the river with another like itself, he came upon a lodge, everything seemingly in place, but, so far as he could see, deserted.

He pulled to the roadside and got out. The air was cold and rarified, but wonderfully pure, even ethereal. In the growing darkness clouds had swept across half the sky, but across the highway he could still trace the willow-bordered river wandering through the long meadow.

He entered a room on the second floor, where the door stood slightly ajar. The bed was made, everything was in order. As he undressed and climbed into bed, he felt that he had climbed to the top of the world. He had climbed to the top of the world and there in the mountains and sky at the end of the day was an unlighted lodge with its door ajar and a clean bed inside, waiting in darkness for him.

18

He awoke to the sound of water running from the eaves of the lodge. From his window he could see that snow had fallen in the night and spread itself lightly over the roof, but now the sky had cleared and the day was radiant.

He drove out into the shining day. In the high green mountains the water had begun to run, seeping over granite walls where moss was clinging, tumbling in white torrents down every crevice, and somewhere in the forest up the steep cliff above him a bird was singing, a rare enchanting sound. He had quite forgotten what it was to be in the high mountains in the season of the early earth.

At twilight he descended again and arrived in the ghost of a small mining town halfway down the far side of the mountains. He could not resist the call of evening, the spring air and the fading light. He walked down a street until he came to the bridge where the darkening river roared, the only noise in the town. Then he strolled quietly on the moonlit streets and surveyed the dark houses and the stars above them.

He had come down from the high mountains in the clear light where a bird was singing, and he wanted to sleep in a house on a shadowy street, to lay his body in a dark cool house and dream with the roar of the dark river in his head.

19

In the dream, he stood beside a little stream on a mountainside, on the green shoulder of a mountain that raised its snow-laden head high in the spring light. Flowers and grass moved in the wind, and the water caught light and spoke with the mouths of stones. He stood entranced. Never, he knew somehow, would there be earth and light for him to love like this again.

And then he saw what he was meant to see. It moved downstream from above like a speck of darkness, like a cinder, an ash, then a cloud in the shining water. It swirled around him swiftly, too quickly, and disappeared downstream. And with it, he barely had time to know, the stream of light that had run through his body was gone forever.

Momentary Lives

IVE ME A HIGHWAY IN HIGH MESA COUNTRY, A ROAD THAT rises and dissolves in sky, that climbs and seeks the light. Such roads there are. Backroads wild and lonely, they are not something imposed upon the landscape so much as something indigenous to it. Their borders are a wilderness of wildflower, light-reflecting, and they traverse high plains to no place as lovely as the roads themselves, forgotten paths the spirit travels. Such roads there are, in such a country, for in such a country I have lived if I have lived at all. Traveling there, one wakes at last to life.

Seeking reprieve, feeling old and full of doubt, I left the city late in summer, headed northerly toward that other country. By afternoon I cleared Raton Pass, and passing through the town of Trinidad, in Colorado, veered northeasterly to nowhere in particular. Something in me began to sing. Before me stretched the world I'd come to see: a vast expanse of mesa, the thread of road, indigenous, a tower of cumulus gathering in a sky light-stricken, cobalt, interminable. At last, the signs of the season were stirring in the very pit of my heart.

By nightfall I was walking the sidewalks in the little town of La Junta—give me a sidewalk on the high side of town, almost abandoned now, overgrown, pushed into unwitnessed upheaval by weed and rabbit brush and seedling elm. Below me lay the Arkansas, cottonwood-bordered. Away to the east, beyond even where heat lightning played in the darkening sky, I recalled that in my youth, in my army days, I'd crossed a bridge in Arkansas and stopped to watch that river. Later in life I'd followed it west, too, twisting my way along a highway through rock-strewn canyons that took me near its source. I'd emerged at the top of the world, thinking all the beautiful places in the world are the lonely places.

It would be a long, impossible story to say how I arrived at that. But if it helps, I remember once, driving west out of Gunnison, approaching a young man walking at his own good pace ahead of me. It was a lonely place, very early in the summer morning, and the world was shining.

I slowed. He was a young black man, strong and light of foot and heart. He shouldered a knapsack and wore remarkably white trousers, and his healthy young chest bulged beneath a striped blue T-shirt. I slowed and thought of stopping, but he was oblivious of me—a glance at his face, as I looked back, told me that. I drove slowly on. Eyes raised, lips slightly parted, he strode like a man reprieved into the shining summer world, a moment of which, at least, we must have shared. We'd headed west out of Gunnison, from the top of the world down the back-bone of a continent, in that brilliant morning light together, and for the rest of my life, the life he'd shared a moment with, I knew he'd live in my memory.

Days, weeks, I wandered northerly. Hastelessly, I doubled

back on backroads, went out of my way to out-of-the-way places I might otherwise have missed forever. On the airy, austere plains of Wyoming I turned westward. In Laramie one Saturday afternoon I sat waiting my turn in a barbershop, braving the close, tobacco-laden air because I was absorbed in watching the people. My turn came last, when the shop had emptied and long shadows had fallen in the street. The barber moved to lock his door, but before he could turn the bolt a final customer entered.

He was no one I knew, surely, or had ever known—of that I'm certain. His heavy shoes, bibbed denim overalls and faded blue shirt attested he was a working man—a laborer on some ranch, I surmised, in from those windy plains with little time to spare. When he sat, his left hand began a patient kneading of his right shoulder. His right, fallen limp upon his lap, revealed the stumps of two missing fingers. Bone tired, he'd doubtless worked all day—with few exceptions, one could see, all the days of his life. On his quiet, perspiring brow the hair had receded slightly, but his dusty face was no betrayer of his age, masked as it was with weariness. His thoughtful glance was courteously averted, and his eyes were dreaming.

But when the barber turned me away in the chair, the eyes met mine for a moment in the mirror I was facing. No, he was no one I knew, surely, yet in that momentary confrontation he helped me see myself, his eyes imparting momentary knowledge of the life I might have lived, the life of the man with the fingers missing, the life of the bone-tired man who comes last of all to the shop in the street where shadows are fallen. Before he turned away again, I'd seen in his eyes a look of obvious curiosity, but curiosity grounded with a strangely mingled peace. Not challenging, almost compassionate, the eyes had merely meant to question, and then had turned again to dream in peace, a peace that flowered in the ground of sheer exhaustion.

Days later, I turned south to drive through Utah, a country full of Biblical-sounding names where I always felt myself a stranger. It was autumn by then. Of a Sunday, I drove through desert and mountain and picked up the wanderings of the Sevier River.

At the near edge of Kanab, a village where mountain and desert meet, I stopped for fuel at a self-service station I thought I'd seen before. A woman, raven-haired, sat by the door and watched as I handled the pump. Serene as the afternoon she moved in, she stood, walked to the car and began cleaning its windshield. She wore sandals, remarkably white levi's, a man's blue polo shirt that flattered a tall, full figure. In the autumn afternoon on the edge of the village at the mouth of the mountains we were alone together, and when I came around the car she stood there faintly smiling. She was beautiful. She seemed the soul of a moment shared in a lonely, incomparably beautiful place.

She was the wife of the station owner. She didn't explain, we didn't exchange a word, but her smile told me that, and told me she knew that I'd driven all day on a lonely road with my heart in my throat because the day was lovely and windless and serene and the year was dying, and that an hour from then, with darkness falling, I'd be gone. She stood there smiling faintly, and, on an impulse, I envied the lives of all who shared her life.

Still, I too had shared it, momentarily. I'll never forget. She was beautiful. I see her standing there smiling, a last, late flower in the night I am driving through toward a place called home.

Typesetting in Goudy Old Style by
G & S, AUSTIN

Printing on Warren's 60 lb. natural by
EDWARDS BROTHERS, ANN ARBOR

Binding by
EDWARDS BROTHERS

Design by
WHITEHEAD & WHITEHEAD, AUSTIN